PENGUIN BOOKS

THE BLOOD OF THE LAMB

Peter De Vries was born in Chicago of Dutch immigrant parents and was educated in Dutch Reformed Calvinist schools. He was graduated from Calvin College in 1931 and for a short time held the post of editor of a community newspaper in Chicago. He then supported himself with a number of different jobs, including those of vending-machine operator, toffee-apple salesman, radio actor, furniture mover, lecturer to women's clubs, and associate editor of *Poetry*. In 1943 he managed to lure James Thurber to Chicago to give a benefit lecture for *Poetry*, and Thurber suggested that De Vries should write for *The New Yorker*. He did. Before long he was given a part-time editorial position on that magazine, dropped his other activities, and moved to New York City. He has remained on the editorial staff of *The New Yorker* ever since. Peter De Vries is the author of some twenty novels, the most recent being *Sauce for the Goose*, also published by Penguin Books. In addition, Penguin publishes his *Consenting Adults, or The Duchess Will Be Furious*; *Forever Panting*; *Madder Music*; and *The Tunnel of Love*. Mr. De Vries lives in Westport, Connecticut, with his wife, Katinka Loeser.

by Peter De Vries

The Blood of
the Lamb

by Peter De Vries

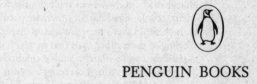

PENGUIN BOOKS

Penguin Books Ltd, Harmondsworth,
Middlesex, England
Penguin Books, 625 Madison Avenue,
New York, New York 10022, U.S.A.
Penguin Books Australia Ltd, Ringwood,
Victoria, Australia
Penguin Books Canada Limited, 2801 John Street,
Markham, Ontario, Canada L3R 1B4
Penguin Books (N.Z.) Ltd, 182–190 Wairau Road,
Auckland 10, New Zealand

First published in the United States of America by
Little, Brown and Company, Inc., 1961
First published in Canada by
Little, Brown and Company (Canada) Limited 1961
Published in Penguin Books by arrangement with
Little, Brown and Company, Inc., 1982

LIBRARY OF CONGRESS CATALOGING IN PUBLICATION DATA
De Vries, Peter.
The blood of the lamb.
Reprint. Originally published: Boston: Little, Brown, 1961.
I. Title.
[PS3507.E8673B5 1982] 813'.52 82–7490
ISBN 0 14 00.6297 1   AACR2

Printed in the United States of America by
R. R. Donnelley & Sons Company, Harrisonburg, Virginia
Set in Linotype Electra

To Jan, Jonny and Derek

The Blood of
the Lamb

one

MY FATHER was not an immigrant in the usual sense of the term, not having emigrated from Holland, so to speak, on purpose. He sailed from Rotterdam intending merely to visit some Dutch relatives and friends who *had* settled in America, but on the way over suffered such ghastly seasickness that a return voyage was unthinkable. He lay for a week in steerage while the worst storm in recent Atlantic memory flung him about his bed and even to the floor. Faces turned green under scarlet sunburns were his sole unsympathetic company; Italians breathed garlic on him, Germans beer and wine. When at last they disembarked, he fell on his knees and kissed the American soil for no other reason than that it was not open water. To face that again was simply out of the question. He canceled his return passage and sent to the Netherlands for his belongings. Thus was added Ben Wanderhope's bit to that sturdy Old World stock from which this nation has sprung.

For the term "fearless voyager" could, indeed, be applied to my father from an intellectual standpoint. A restless, questing spirit soon had him in seas identifiable, among the Chicago Calvinist Dutch Reformed with whom he sought his portion, as those of Doubt.

"Take the story of the alabaster box of precious ointment," he said one evening to my Uncle Hans, an Iowa clergyman visiting us that summer on what turned out to be a busman's holiday. My uncle ground his teeth; he would greatly have preferred strolling around the block with a cigar in them, amusing the neighborhood children by wiggling his ears, which he could do with amazing virtuosity, one at a time as well as jointly. Especially galling was a believer backslidden from having too diligently searched the Scriptures, as the Scriptures themselves enjoined. "It stands in one Gospel that it happened in the home of a Pharisee in a city called Nain, and that 'a woman who was a sinner' poured it on his feet. In another that it was in Bethany in the home of Simon the leper and that the woman poured it on his head. John says the woman was Mary and that Lazarus was at the table, which it's pretty funny the other writers didn't mention if it's true. One place you read Judas Iscariot objected to the waste, another that all the disciples did. Now if the Bible is infallible how can it contradict itself?"

"The trouble with you, Ben, is . . . how shall I say it?" My uncle paused characteristically for the right words, which he found with characteristic precision. "You strain at a gnat and swallow a camel."

"That was neatly put," my brother called from an adjoining bedroom where he was dressing for a date. Now nineteen, Louie had lost his faith during his medical studies at the University of Chicago. "You have a way with words, Uncle Hans." I was twelve at the time, and unaware of irony, but I can see Louie well enough now, grinning into the bureau glass as he knotted his necktie.

My father comes clearly to mind, too, drinking bootleg whiskey while a steady flow of grimaces contorted his face. His lips puffed and receded, his dense white eyebrows moved up and down and even, I think, sideways, separately maneuverable like my uncle's ears. What was odd, even a trifle sinister, about this constant facial play was that its sequences bore no observable connection with what was being said to him, or even, for that matter, by him, issuing rather — to the extent that one can be sure about such things — from what he was secretly thinking. His features behaved as a man's will who is talking to himself, which, indeed, he did in no small degree, even during the course of conversations.

Neighbors had by now begun to drop in to pay respects to the "dominee" in our midst, staying to watch his performance in this theological first aid and to shower concern on the man who required it. My father reveled in others' pity; he basked in being felt sorry for and in being worried about, with an almost voluptuous pleasure. Believers watched the Doubter with awe as they lifted their cups of coffee, taken in discreet preference to the strong drink, which was in any case offered in a manner designed to ensure rejection: "You don't want a shot, do you, Jake? Naw. You, Herman? Naw." Whenever I read those family reminiscences written by people obviously priding themselves on antecedents of great color, I smile secretly at the memory of my father gargling with bourbon in the winter months as a throat protective; using, for chewing tobacco, cigar stumps from which the charred ends had been scissored; and lubricating the door hinges with oil left over from sardine tins — such was his parsimony.

"The thing we must do," said my uncle, "is ignore the promptings of the Devil — "

"I figured this out myself."

"— who tempts the mind, *och ja*, Ben, as much as the flesh, and we must emulate Christ, who reminds us that things are hidden" — my uncle twisted in his chair to fire this barb into the open bedroom where Louie was dressing — "from the wise and prudent and revealed unto babes and sucklings."

"Neatly put" came again archly from in there.

"How about me?" my father said, resenting any shift in attention from himself. "How about me in doubt and turmoil? That's all well and good, Hans, but what I'm trying to say is, one error in the Bible and the doctrine of infallibility goes to pieces. It's all or nothing."

"Then take it all, Ben," my uncle said. "We must put away the pride of the flesh, of which the reason is a part, and accept salvation as we accept a mystery. For he who finds himself shall lose himself, and he who loses himself shall find himself. Like I said Sunday."

"And the virgin birth. We get that in a chapter where the lineage is traced through Joseph. How can those two things be true?"

"The virgin birth business was slipped in by a later writer, prolly, after the doctrine had been cooked up by the church," said Louie, joining us.

A gasp went around the kitchen table, at which now a small congregation sat. Men stiffened in their black

6

suits, and women shook their heads as heresy darkened into blasphemy. Here under one roof were two candidates for the dread *afgescheidenen*, a term as dire as "purge" to citizens of a later absolutism. My mother poured coffee with a trembling hand; my nearly blind grandmother, who lived with us at the time, was busily trying to sweep cigar burns in the oilcloth into a crumber; my grandfather went out to the front porch, where he stood scratching himself in a manner said to be depreciating property values. My uncle shook a finger threateningly in Louie's face. "I'll pray for you."

"Do dat," said Louie, whose Chicago street diction was being but slowly refined by influences on the University Midway.

"That damnable school where they teach you such things."

"Pa get his from there? We can read for ourselves, is the thing, and I'll tell you this about the Bible. You don't have to believe it's infallible to get something out of it, in fact it's only after you've dropped all that *geklets* that you can begin to appreciate it as great literature."

A special murmur of dismay was excited by this, for the heresy that the Bible was great literature was one the clergy were trying particularly to spike. Dr. Berkenbosch, who had just arrived to look in on my grandmother, stood flattened against the kitchen door, his eyes closed but rolling under their lids as well we knew, wishing he had not come. "Next he'll call Thy word poetry," my uncle said. "He's going to call it gracefully written. Forgive him, O Lord, I ask it in advance."

"The Book of Job is the greatest drama ever struck

7

off by the hand of man. Just terrific theater. Greater than Aeschylus, prolly."

"Down on our knees, shall we, everyone, and try yet to pluck this brand from the burning?"

The hearers were too stricken to move from their chairs, in which they stiffened as though charges of electric current were being passed through their frames. Moans ran around the table, heads were shaken.

"He says it's great drama. Sheer theater — God's word. *Hemelse Vader.*"

Whatever the theater in Job, there was no lack of it in our kitchen that night. Above the Greek chorus of Dutch lamentations could be heard my brother exclaiming, "It's your silly theologies that have made religion impossible and mucked up people's lives till you can't call it living any more! Look at Ma! Look at Pa!"

Look at them indeed. Our mother was wiping the table with one hand and her eyes with the other. Our father had his elbows on the table and seemed to be trying to extricate his head from his hands as from a porthole, or vise, into which it had been inadvertently thrust. My uncle put his face up close to Louie's and said, "You're talking to a servant of God!"

"You're talking to someone who hasn't let the brains God gave him rot, and doesn't intend to!"

Such a scene may seem, to households devoid of polemic excitement, to lie outside credulity, but it was a common one in ours. Now when I am myself no longer assailed by doubts, being rather lashed by certainties, I can look back on it with a perspective quite lacking in my view of it then, for my teeth were chattering. We were a chosen people, more so than the Jews, who had "rejected the cornerstone," our concept of Calvinist election reinforced by that of Dutch supremacy. My mother even then sometimes gave the impression that she thought Jesus was a Hollander. Not that our heroes did not include men of other extractions and other faiths. Several years after the Scopes trial, we were still aggressively mourning the defeat of William Jennings Bryan, and it took very little time for the subject of evolution to come into the argument.

"What about a First Cause?" my uncle said. "Where did the world come from if God didn't make it?"

"What about vestigial organs?" my brother countered. "The only reason you can wiggle your ears better than the rest of us is the muscles left over from the olden days haven't atrophied as much as most people's. You've also got a set to swing a tail with, pal, take it from me. Not to speak of over a hundred other remnants from wisdom teeth to hair you've got no use for now but once retained body heat for four-footed beasts."

"Down on our knees, shall we?"

"We've been through that stage."

"Why haven't I got a tail, if I've still got the muscles to wag it?"

"Don't think you once didn't. Which brings us to the embryo, if vestigial organs don't convince you. Do you know what 'ontogeny recapitulates phylogeny' means?"

"I am not impressed by big words," said my uncle, who was always ready enough to bandy "predestination" and "infralapsarianism."

"Means the individual enacts in miniature the entire evolutionary history of the race, beginning with con-

9

ception." Louie turned to my aunt, who happened to be conveniently pregnant. "How far along is Aunt Wilhelmina here?"

"Will you shut your foul mouth?"

"Seven months? Then the gill clefts her kid had at two — a relic of the fish stage, you see — are closed up. The breathing apparatus of land animals has developed, pal. The notochord has become the vertebrate spine. Your kid has its feet curled in toward each other, sweetheart, like hands, capable of grasping branches. The tail it has had all these months will by birth have withered away, though occasionally a human mammal is born with one. You can talk yourself blue in the face, but you and Bryan and Billy Sunday and anybody else you care to name are walking museums of what you deny, while Aunt Wilhelmina is carrying inside her a synopsis of the story thus far. Your child is about to come down out of the trees."

My uncle turned and, for a moment, seemed to shift his protest to his wife, or at least to evaluate her with new eyes, as one capable of betraying his most cherished principles and possibly even threatening their livelihood in thus carting about in her middle a digest of Natural Selection. Louie hurried on.

"More dramatic throwbacks are harelips harking back to piscine ancestors with that nostril formation, dog-faced boys seen in circus sideshows — "

Here a shriek from my aunt herself brought an abrupt change in the course events had thus far taken. Running from the room, she cried, "Wat scheelt u?" (What ails you?) "Talking about those things in front of a woman who's carrying!" Several women hurried into the parlor behind her, poor choices to calm hysteria since they shared all too keenly the peasant superstitions from which it sprang, and were in a few instances in a delicate condition themselves.

Suddenly the whole house was a boiling uproar. People ran back and forth from kitchen to parlor like victims of a panic with no leader. Hands soothed my heaving aunt, loosening her clothes so she could breathe, or were simply wrung to the accompaniment of rolled eyes and deploring clucks. Doc Berkenbosch seized his bag and flew into the parlor, closing the door after pushing all the men and some of the women back into the passage like a subway attendant. My uncle wheeled on Louie.

"You! I'm surprised at you, a so-called educated person, knowing no better than to talk like that in front of a woman in the family way. Is that what they teach you at the University, how to bring dog-faced boys and so on into the world?"

"But people don't believe those old wives' tales about marked babies any more." The feminine chorus rising beyond the closed door to some extent belied this assumption. "Those are just foolish superstitions we ought to help women be free of. We no longer believe in prenatal influence."

"No longer — !" My uncle stood aghast. "What have you just been telling us but that? Cleft palates, donkey ears, tails — it's all there, you just got through saying, waiting for an unguarded word or evil influence to bring it out. It's all there, science tells us. Aunt Wilhelmina's got the makings of any kind of freak you care to name inside her. Name it and she's got it, you said."

"That's not what I said. I said that everybody is a

walking museum of evolution, and it's up to you to explain the fact if Genesis is true and God created man on Saturday as a land animal. I mean what kind of God would create something to be a land biped and then stuff him with relics of a marine past and a crawling past and a quadruped past he never had? How do you explain that? I mean I'm curious."

My uncle wagged an unlighted cigar warningly in Louie's face. "If I have an albino — "

The door burst open and Doc Berkenbosch galloped into view, his coat off and rolling up his shirtsleeves. "Water," he said, "get me some water," and galloped back again.

Someone snatched up a kettle and filled it at the sink while another struck a match to light the gas stove. These were of the more liberal, or enlightened, element who attended movies in face of the church's ban on that form of entertainment. "She's going to have it here. It's been brought on," one said. The kitchen table was cleared; somebody began tearing his shirt into strips for bandages.

"No, no, a *glass* of water," said the returned Doc Berkenbosch. "To take a sedative with." He was given a tumblerful, with which he trotted back again into the parlor.

Through the door now left open we could see my aunt in a straight chair gulping down the pill, while Doc Berkenbosch's stethoscope rode the white billows of her bosom. The women in attendance, most of them as fat as she, formed a ring of Corybants about an Earth Mother they had husked down to the waist. Handkerchiefs soaked in strong cologne were offered her as restoratives, whiffs of which reached us in the passage where we stood craning our necks. At last Doc put his stethoscope by and announced that she would neither "have it here" nor require further concern provided rubbernecking curiosity and rival ministrations — such as the toilet waters at war with his tranquilizer — did not defeat his own. The women kept up a steady low sound neither cooing nor lamentation, but both. My mother smote her temples softly in the middle distance. A neighbor addicted to opening the Bible at random for guidance in times of stress took ours from the shelf and read aloud into the din, "Moab is my washpot; over Edom will I cast out my shoe," without noticeably bringing order out of chaos. Order was restored only after Doc had reassumed the guise of subway attendant and pushed everybody, men *and* women, into the kitchen. Here my father's voice was heard calling us back to the fundamentals from which we had so flamboyantly strayed.

"How about me in perdition? How about my doubts about the, *och ja*, whole Bible, not just Genesis? *I say there is no hell.* Now do you believe I'll burn in it? Now do you understand how serious this is, and we better get busy?"

But now my uncle had bigger fish to fry. He awaited impatiently the return of Doc Berkenbosch from the front bedroom, where Doc had gone to look in on the person he had originally come to see, my grandmother, who had been forced to lie down as a result of the to-do. When Doc walked in at last, one could tell from his face that he knew what was coming, and how much he dreaded it. He hated umpiring these arguments between

Faith and Reason in a community where, God knew, it was his church connections rather than his medical skills that kept him his practice.

"Dr. Berkenbosch," my uncle instantly began, "you've been to medical school. Is there anything to what Louie here has been telling us?"

"We-ell . . ."

Smiling at the floor and pinching his nose, Doc spoke of the embryos in their jars in the old biology lab, the frog specimens floating in formaldehyde and the acids in the test tubes, all mingling their smells into one pungent essence, which he could remember still, and which was far more capable of provoking tears of nostalgia for his alma mater than glee clubs with their voices raised in song or ivy on a wall. He recalled some of his professors, the jokes they'd played on them, the fun they'd had in those days that were gone forever but that could be relived in memory yet. Then he glanced at the clock and said, "Goodness, I've got another call to make tonight. Maternity case too. Well, good-by, all," and snatched up his bag and fled.

I after him. Doc, with whom I was on friendly terms, often took me along on house calls in his old Reo, and he was certainly not averse to having a kid riding beside him tonight after all that adult commotion. Stimulated by what I had just seen and heard, however, I had no intention of giving him any peace.

"Doc," I said, after we had bumped along for a block or two, "is there anything to all that? That we're all those other animals first before we get born?"

Doc threw a harried glance over his shoulder preparatory to turning a corner. "Well, no matter what there's in there, we'll get it out, thanks to medical science. The strides we've made! Sometimes it takes a little doing, instruments and one thing and another, but we pull them through oftener than not."

"Gills and tails and so on. What about them?"

Doc was encouraging about all that. He said a lot could be done for even the most difficult cases; that fetuses might be ever so incomplete and malformed, but given time, proper nourishment and prenatal care, at the end of nine months, which was all medical science asked, medical science would lay a fine, healthy child in its mother's arms. "We call those full-term pregnancies," he explained, "and you'd be surprised the strides we're making in getting them. The woman I'm going to call on right now has got a youngster in a turned-around position, I don't mind informing you, just between us," he said as we drew to a stop before a red-brick bungalow. "We call that a breech delivery."

"What will you do?"

"Tell her."

"Could any of these things be happening because they're fallen women?" I asked, drawing on another of the clichés we were given like a quiverful of arrows with which to face a life cursed by sin.

Doc sat a moment with his hand on the door handle before getting out. "Well, now, it's interesting that you ask. I had a woman recently who fell, not just one flight of stairs, but two. She had a baby as perfect as a pool ball."

"How long before the birth did she fall?"

"Ten months, maybe a year. But it didn't interfere

with her conception none, and the child that I laid in her arms, as I say, was perfect in every respect."

"How could she fall down two flights of stairs?"

"Well, it was one of the miracles of medicine. She fell down one flight to the landing, *turned left and rolled down another flight*, clear to the ground floor, sir. She laid there in the hall till she picked herself up and walked away, and no broken bones or organic damage either. It was one of the wonders of my practice, I can tell you."

"Would you accept a patient with gills and a tail — proving evolution?"

"We turn no one away. Not even," Doc added, citing an even greater monstrosity, "when they can't pay."

Sitting alone in the car while Doc made his call, I pondered all that I had heard that evening, of faith in mysteries shaken by mysteries as great if not greater; of miracles supplanted by scientific fact as conducive to reverence as the miracles. I thought I understood now the helplessness of newborn babes: they were weak, not because they were infants or tiny, but because they had just got through recapitulating a billion years of evolution. Enough to tucker anybody out!

These mysteries more or less settled, or at least tabled, in my mind, I spent the return trip querying Doc about my father, a man given to the operatic recital of ailments no less baffling than the phenomena discussed.

"Ben's internal complaints are not unusual for a man with his bum insides," Doc said. "Take his stomach. It's not the best, but whether he's suffering from ulsters or not we can't say yet. But he's certainly the ulster type, and should cut out the liquor. I'd appreciate your talking to him about that. It helps nervousness keep the stomach in an upset condition, causing the acid digestive juices to eat perforations in the wall, usually at the point where it empties into the plethora . . . "

It will need no saying that Doc Berkenbosch's endowments were of the sketchiest, to put it mildly. While some of his terminologies could charitably be laid to embedment in a community where pronunciations were at best loosely colloquial — we all of us there said "ulsters" and "arthuritis" — some could not, but must be attributed to his abysmal training. He had gone to one of the worst medical schools in the country at a time when medical schools were a scandal. The situation was cleaned up around 1910; since then there have been no such things as unaccredited medical colleges, but there were when he got his diploma on some Southeastern campus or other and was launched into a waiting world. Strides though medical science may have made, Doc was always lengthening or shortening his own to avoid recipients of his services on the street. He had set a broken leg for another aunt of mine in a cast two inches short, so that she walked with a limp and a cane the rest of her life, which, thanks to her switching physicians, was a fairly long one. His boner — how grotesquely apt the term is! — left her undaunted and not really embittered; she took it, peasant-fashion, as part of the misfortune that had visited her in the first place. I had a bad turn some years later when I learned that my own birth had occurred unexpectedly in the house, with Doc officiating, under conditions very possibly like those adumbrated by the movie-goers who were so ready to boil water and improvise dressings from the shirts off their backs.

The women were sitting quietly in the parlor when I got home, my aunt the center of a clucking circle, placidly turning the pages of our family album. Child after child with the requisite number of fingers and toes and bearing no noticeable taint of imbecility was loitered over, to balance and cancel out any evil released from the hint that she might be carrying a Pleistocene freak under her heart. The men were in the kitchen less composedly discussing Total Depravity, a tenet for some reason always especially dear to our folk. My uncle was explaining its connection with Original Sin, taking himself as an example to say that, while conceding he had character, integrity, a keen mind and a gift for scholarship second to none, he was unworthy in his own eyes and in the eyes of God, all his works as naught and his righteousness as filthy rags. This being our view of human merit, it can be imagined what we thought of vice. I sat huddled over folded arms and shivering again as I listened to estimates of the curse laid by the Fall on humankind, a curse thanks to which "the whole creation groaneth and travaileth in pain together" — a blight to which could be attributed all the ills that vex our mortal lot: madness and murder, lust, blasphemy, disease, rape, incest, and skies of gray. My father had evidently had his fill of provoked alarm, at least for the time being, and was content to sit and listen, albeit rather dramatically. With an effect of taking the Fall personally, he began twisting his bandanna in his horny fists and giving play to facial contortions like a man running through a series of expressions in a frantic search for the right one.

My uncle reached out a hand of his own to stay the scene-stealing and its attendant eternal mugging. "Never mind that. God doesn't want outward display. He wants us to — *och ja*, how shall I put it?" There was an especially long pause while the right words were groped for. "To rend our hearts and not our garments."

"You certainly have a way with language, Hans. You can certainly hit the nail on the head," said my father, whose familiarity with Holy Writ was perhaps not as great as my uncle need have feared.

Between these two groups sat my mother silently poring over her beloved rock collection — the unsung saint and unsuspected villain of the whole works. For in that innocent hobby lurked something far more traitorous to our world and life view than my father's doubts and my brother's iconoclasm. It was not until years afterward that I thought in those terms of the scene which ended that long night.

When the last caller had left, my uncle sat down to draft at white heat some notes for a sermon inspired by the evening's events. Its text was the first verse of Genesis, and it was to be a treatise on the exact age of the earth, as deduced from chronologies of the Old and New Testaments and other reliable sources to be six thousand years. He worked at a parlor table overflowing, as did many another piece of furniture, with my mother's beloved specimens — talismans from her Dutch birthplace carried across the sea, souvenirs of every vacation taken in this country and every walk along the Lake Michigan beach. I sat nearby, permitted to watch.

"There," said my uncle, when his pencil had raced to a flourishing stop. He evened the manuscript pages together, then looked for a paperweight to keep them from blowing away in the summer breeze that rustled the curtains at the open window. He selected, of course, one of my mother's minerals. It was a piece of fossil from the Paleozoic era, five hundred million years old.

two

FOR A LONG TIME my father had insomnia, and so was let sleep till all hours. "Shh" was the first word I learned, and as an injunction aimed at me, not at others on my infant behalf, and walking on tiptoe my first conception of human locomotion, gained through the slats of my crib.

After retiring at a conventional enough hour, my father would lie wide-eyed until dawn, when he would sink into a slumber lasting until noon. This gave him a tenure of sixteen hours between the sheets and eight out, more or less reversing the normal human ratio. He had an ice route with a partner named Wigbaldy, Dutch-born like himself, who bore the brunt of this dislocation, carrying on alone until with the sun high in the sky my father would appear in one or another of the Chicago alleys up which they plied their trade with horse and wagon, or what was more likely, overtake Wigbaldy at one of the many saloons they serviced, at least until Prohibition, ready for the day's first refreshment. Like most

21

insomniacs, he resented any implication that he had slept well or, indeed, at all.

Numerous reasons were given for my father's disturbance, which continued intermittently for years and survived two business partners. One was his hankerings for his homeland, another those religious doubts, and still another, worry over what Louie might be up to while he tossed and turned. Since it was into my own bed that Louie crept at last, full of tales, his nocturnal exploits were known to me long before I was of an age to give concern on that score myself. He took his girls into the bushes of Chicago's splendid park system, there to pursue his advantage with excerpts from Shelley and Swinburne recited in the accents of the streets off which he had lured them:

> As, when late larks give warning
> Of dying lights and dawning,
> Night murmurs to de morning,
>   "Lie still, O love, lie still;"
> And half her dark limbs cover
> De light limbs of her lover,
> Wit' amorous plumes dat hover
>   And fervent lips dat chill.

Add to these assorted apprehensions the anxiety my mother never ceased expressing over my habit of sleeping with Louie. I was always a delicate child, while he had never been sick a day in his life, and everyone knew what happened when two people of such unequal constitutions shared the same bed: the stronger drained away the vitality of the weaker.

The opinions of someone who thought Christ was a Hollander were not to be taken lightly. They were the more formidable for a thousand years of European credence behind them, as was the case with the conviction about the sleeping arrangement. My mother forcibly broke it up several times, driving me into the small spare room vacated by my grandparents whenever they left us for a turn in another of the filial households among which they systematically rotated; or what was oftener the case, making me stay there after having been banished to it for the duration of an illness. In the end I always stole back, sometimes in the dead of night, to the brother I adored. Then after a few more months the cry for segregation would be revived. The seven-year gap in our ages meant a disadvantage in size, increasing the certainty that my vigor was being nightly sapped away. And indeed I went from measles to mumps (diagnosed by thrusting a pickle into the suspect's mouth and observing his facial reaction) to scarlet fever to yellow jaundice to God knows what all. We were quarantined four times and fumigated twice. My slender frame and precarious bloodstream seemed a catchall for every malady obtainable.

The thing for which I was perhaps best suited was pneumonia. I had three or four bouts of that, none serious, and each equipping me to throw off its successor with greater ease — the blessed paradox of the sickly. Of its counterpart, the man who "never had a sick day in his life" and has therefore accumulated no antibodies, my brother was destined to give tragic proof.

One raw winter day in his twentieth year, Louie came home from the University with a terrible chill. He shook as he undressed and climbed into bed. We had no thermometer, and it was not until Doc Berkenbosch arrived that evening that we learned he had a fever of a hundred and three and a half. Doc stowed his stethoscope away with no more than his usual sobriety and a casual, "Got a mean chest cold there, boy." But after leaving the bedroom, he beckoned us into the sitting room and said, "I think I'll stay a while. Vrouw Wanderhope, how about a cup coffee?"

Now I had to sleep in the spare room because Louie was sick, a strange and disquieting novelty. Far into the uneasy night I could hear the grownups murmuring in the adjacent living room. The smells of tobacco and coffee seeped under my closed door. I was awake when Doc left at midnight and awake when he returned at dawn.

All that day and the next, Saturday and Sunday, I knew Louie's life hung by a thread. The word "crisis" quivered like an arrow in my heart. On Sunday afternoon, having looked in on Louie again, Doc dropped the words "both lungs." The minister was summoned after evening service, to conduct a devotional in our house. He read a Psalm, and then everyone knelt at his chair to pray. We had the customary "parlor suit" of the period — a sofa and two Cogswell chairs embroidered in romantic or woodland scenes. The face of a shepherd boy smiled at me through the patterns of a crocheted white tidy as I stared through my fingers, not praying so much as listening to the prayer. The words "life everlasting" dropped from ministerial lips were my first intimation of mortality.

My sensation, rather than fear or piety, was a baffled and uncomprehending rage. That flesh with which I had lain in comradely embrace destroyable, on such short notice, by a whim known as divine? By what authority and to what authority must this sleek version of the routed Uncle Hans plead for the life of a lad as beguiling as the shepherd grinning at me by the needlework river? Who wantonly scattered such charm, who broke such flesh like bread for his purposes? In later years, years which brought me to another such vigil over one more surely my flesh and blood, I came to understand a few things about what people believe. What people believe is a measure of what they suffer. "The Lord giveth and the Lord taketh away" — there must be balm of some sort in that for men whose treasures have been confiscated. These displaced Dutch fisherfolk, these farmers peddling coal and ice in a strange land, must have had their reasons for worshiping a god scarcely distinguishable from the devil they feared. But the boy kneeling on the parlor floor was shut off from such speculatory solaces. All the theologies inherent in the minister's winding drone came down to this: Believe in God and don't put anything past him. Or another thought formed itself in the language of the streets in which the boy had learned crude justice and mercy: *"Why doesn't He pick on somebody his size?"*

It was in vain that I strove to feel anything like a sense of prayer. My thoughts were like the smoke of Cain's altar fire, imagined as not ascending. Yet being unable to pray for Louie was loyalty to Louie, whose disciple I had early been. I remembered a church entertainment of which one of the numbers had been a monologue condensed from a Christmas legend by Henry van Dyke entitled "The Lost Word." It was about a well-born youth of ancient Antioch who backslides from Christianity, bartering the name of God for worldly ease in a kind of Faustian bargain with a pagan priest in the Grove of Daphne, into which he has wandered seeking respite for his spirit. When after some years his little son lies at the point of death, he cannot pray for the boy's life, having forfeited the Name in which alone supplication can be made. The piece was a favorite dear to local spellbinders who gripped their audiences with lines like: "The roses bloomed and fell in the garden; the birds sang and slept among the jasmine-bowers. But in the heart of Hermas there was no song." His old teacher, John of Antioch, reappears at the critical moment with the word he has forgotten, then at last Hermas can pray for his son, and . . . "Was it an echo? It could not be, for it came again — the voice of the child, clear and low, waking from sleep, and calling: 'My father, my father!' " In the applause that burst over the retiring elocutionist, Louie had turned to me and whispered, "Pure hokum." It was the first time I had heard the word, but its meaning was instantly clear to me, hitching up my standards with a force that opened vistas, that made me laugh and nod even as I clapped madly with eyes full of tears — tears left over from the preceding period, that of gullibility, or unsophistication, from which I had just abruptly graduated.

What would Louie have thought of the scene being enacted in his behalf now? I turned to steal a glance at my parents. My father was making faces appropriate to supplication behind his hairy hands. His mugging seemed a shade more human, now, though perhaps also slightly less sane. The smell of bourbon mingled with the mystic fumes of prayer. His suspenders were unhooked and hung down in two festoons in a manner that made my mind leap prophetically forward from all this to another life I knew awaited me. This was the "worldly" life denounced by the church, in which Louie had briefly walked and toward which I would in due course set my feet. What I felt, like a bubble of anticipation bursting in a sea of grief, is perhaps difficult to explain to anyone except in terms of some other such anarchic childhood vision of his own: a window opened on the world, an apocalyptic flash, very likely all nothing more than lyric expressions of the plan to Get Away from Home. In my case it included the special pains of a boy chafing under an immigrant culture, for whom "wider horizons" meant those from the advantage of which people shouted at you on the street:

> Oh, the Irish and the Dutch
> Don't amount to very much.

My father's habits and appearance excited in me this desire for a more fashionable world. The houses around the Midway where Louie went to school embodied it.

My mother was another story. Her head was bowed, but under the bony hands I knew the face, gray as the hair that framed it, was a mask. Fear for the moment kept every other emotion at bay. Till it was time, *Moeke*, as Louie had always affectionately continued to call her, would give no sign. Then she would pluck her hair out by the roots.

The easy rote of the minister's words faltered as the prayer took a more portentous turn.

"We know that this child of grace, this son of the Covenant, has in his youth expressed doubts of Thy

. . . Grant that in this hour . . . may yet be time . . . remission of his sins in Jesus' name. Amen."

Rising from the floor was a rustling reintrusion of the physical, absurdly fatal to the spiritual mood we sought. We seemed more insignificant on our feet than kneeling — pathetic seekers after what the very strain of seeking seemed to disperse. The minister wheezed a little, and I could not keep my mind off the muscles for wagging a bygone tail on which it was Louie's story that he now sat. Only for a moment, however. After such a prayer he must go in to see Louie, more directly to pursue the hope expressed in it. Nobody could have found fault with the way he did this.

A doctor's "no visitors" order was not taken to include pastoral calls, and anyhow the question of not disturbing Louie was academic now, since he had been in a near-coma for some hours. He did not seem aware of the minister slipping in, and the rest of us after him, to range ourselves in a hushed row at the foot of the brass bed.

Louie's golden head was rolled away from us, toward the wall. His curls were a damp tangle, his brow beaded with sweat. He breathed through his mouth, irregular gasps that strained his throat and reached the vain destination of his lungs with great laboring heaves. My mother wiped his forehead with a handkerchief, and after that we all watched with inclined heads, and that expression of gentle, hopeless love with which human dying is witnessed. Louie snored on. Once he stirred and mumbled something that sounded like "No problem of mine." From far down the street came the sound of a grind organ trolling out the intermezzo from *Cavalleria Rusticana*.

Doc was with us, and something in Louie's breathing made him push his way forward with his stethoscope, that useless prop. He shook his head after listening through it, and stepped back again. Then, like something fluidly rehearsed between them many a time, the minister stepped forward. I shall never forget the grace with which he performed his chore.

"It's dot old *klets* again, Louie. Dot old Van Scoyen who bores you, eh, boy? *Och ja, ik ben en kletskous.*" (I am a chatterbox.)

Louie opened one eye, then both, at this. After taking the minister's face in with a prolonged, glassy stare, he nodded once. For a moment, the old ironic grin curled his cracked lips. Van Scoyen wasted no more time.

"We hope you're going to be feeling better tomorrow, old boy, and that you'll be out of this soon. Then you'll have to put up with the old *klets* again. But just now, Louie, I want to ask you. You have expressed doubts. You don't have doubts any more now, eh, *jongen?*"

We stood in a frozen circle, waiting. Louie's face lost its expression, and his head rolled back toward the wall. Fearing he was slipping into unconsciousness again, my mother pressed in and bent closely over him. A long, quivering sigh shook him from head to foot, a moan asking that he be left in peace.

"It's *Moeke*, Louie," she said. "You have no doubts, have you, Louie?"

The rolling motion of his head became a negative shake. He said in an unexpectedly clear voice, "No — no doubts."

A single sigh of relief went through the room. Louie closed his eyes, and we were sure he was gone. Then, as

I watched, I saw them open again and his gaze fix on me, and me alone. The old grin wreathed his lips once more as he said slyly, for just my benefit, "No doubts on my part."

It was the last communication between us. He died about three o'clock that morning with my mother and me in the bedroom, keeping watch beside his bed. We had both dozed, exhausted, in our chairs and, awakened by the sudden silence in the room, saw that Louie had left us.

He had gone at his best, leaving to each what was needed most. To *Moeke*, peace of mind on the terms she required. To me, freedom from uncertainty too — from that faith with whose account of Louie I could not have lived. No more need I go on thinking in anguished rage: "Why doesn't He pick on somebody his size?" "He" did not exist. So Louie had died saying.

My mother did not quite yet give way. She rose and, taking something from the dresser, began to brush his golden hair.

three

AFTER HIS DEATH, Louie remained as much as ever a model to me, or even more, being now idealized in my mind. His life had been of course anything but model by the standards of the household in which his departure had torn so cruel a gash, but all that was to the end successfully kept from *Moeke*. My father continued fluctuating wildly between Faith and Reason, hardly a figure to excite the concern to which he aspired, or even to be taken seriously, being rather like one of those comedians seen hanging from cliffs as they mugged at the depths below, in the films to which we snuck under interdict. I quickly removed from Louie's room all that would have hurt our *Moeke* or reminded her of the days before his feigned conversion: books of an agnostic stripe, snapshots of girls clearly not of the Covenant, some illustrated pamphlets on the "art of love" from a locked cabinet, to which I finally found the key.

Such stuff Louie had himself long since outgrown, but to me, now of the age at which they had come to him in plain wrappers, they were treasures to be again restored to lock and key for later delectation. Between what they told me and what I had learned from Louie's small-hour recitals of his experiences, I was, by the age of sixteen or so, a diligent if not exactly subtle amorist prowling the gravel paths of Hamilton Park in search of "frails" and "cookies." With no better a version of the Chicago street diction than his, I lay — while *Moeke* waited at the window and Pa twisted among the sheets — in the municipal bushes as Louie had, murmuring into some feminine ear:

> Who goes amid de greenwood
> Wit' mien so virginal?

This was Joyce, loosely remembered, from the treasures on Louie's shelf of favorites, recited with the peak of my cap switched around, the better to pursue the erotic sequences with what the handbooks called "technique." I breathed along the girl's cheek what the manuals termed "olfactory kisses," greatly exciting to the female as preparation for more ardent maneuvers. Nowadays when, as one gathers, literary criticism is exchanged among the Radcliffe and Harvard lovers along the Charles, I look back on our own preference for the originals as somehow healthier than practices that, however more cerebral, would, as a means of furthering romantic communion, have struck us as "against nature."

The girl I saw oftenest in my days as a high-school senior was named Maria Italia, whom guilt over our indulgence in the more Arcadian corners of the park kept from asking me in to meet her father, whose austerity had driven us there in any case. We sometimes finished our evenings on the swing on her back porch, when

32

the house was dark and he was presumed in bed. Late one autumn night as we sat there bundled in sweaters, I raised her flannel skirt and contemplated what this action exposed with a regard both fervent and debonair. I French-inhaled the smoke from a cigarette held poised in the other hand. "Sometimes I think this leg is the most beautiful thing in the world, and sometimes the other," I said. "I suppose the truth lies somewhere in between."

A noise made me turn and see in the kitchen window a mustached apparition watching us in clear moonlight, gesticulating with an air of detached, underwater suffering. I was off with the speed of a deer.

I ran the half-mile home, where the counterpart in parental vigil awaited me. I carried my shoes up the inside stairway to the second floor of the frame two-flat where we lived, and hearing a noise behind the closed door, put them on again. I entered with my shoelaces tinkling.

"Hello, *Moeke*," I said, reaching for my cap, to find the peak still behind.

"*Waar ben je toch geweest?*"

"Park."

"What doing?"

"Well, *Moeke*, you're not going to like this. There's a new discussion group that meets in the fieldhouse there, but we discuss current affairs, and God made them too. It's perfectly all right. Go to bed now, *Moeke*."

After kissing her good night, I shot into the bathroom, there to find my father scrubbing his teeth with the washrag, as was his wont. He stood in his long underwear, and the spectacle made blaze anew my dream of high life: of standards and of suavity, certainly dedication to the arts.

"Where were you?"

"Well, Pa —"

The violent application of the washrag to my cheek produced a crimson stain on the cloth. "Outsider?"

"I don't know her name. Well, I think it's Italia."

"What nationality is that?"

"I'm not sure. They're nice people. Dark-complected but nice. Awful strict."

My father slammed the washcloth down into the bowl with a Dutch obscenity it would be folly to try to translate, and shook a finger in my face, being now midway a phase where traditional values were temporarily reaffirmed. "Any girl you go out with you take here, *verstaan*, because I want to see what Jesus would say." He picked up the washcloth to slam it down with another *splat*. "First Louie, now you. No sleep, in bed till noon. One partner dead, another dying on his feet. I tell you I can't stand no more."

I laughed softly as I hurried to my bedroom, a chuckle of affection for origins from which I would soon be gone, had already in spirit flown. I had a vision of polished doors opening, and myself in faultless tweeds in a party moving toward dinner across a parquet floor, under a chandelier like chiseled ice.

Mr. Italia sat belching under a pair of oval-framed photographs of parents hairier, if possible, than himself. His wife was dead, but there was a picture of her, too, in her casket, gazing out at us with an eerie simulacrum of motherly love. Dark-complected Mr. Italia was indeed, with handle-bar mustaches of a size that might have made him topple forward out of his chair were it not for the posture seemingly aimed at correcting the leverage in his favor. He drank beer after thrusting into my hand a bottle of soda pop of marked but unidentifiable flavor, pale yellow in color, and lukewarm. (Back to your tents, O Israel!) On a table beside him was an open bottle of olives, from which he helped himself, at intervals tipping a little of the liquid into a flowerpot to keep its level below that at which he would stain his fingers when fishing for another. He offered the bottle to me, but I declined with a shake of my head. He had been quizzing me for an hour about my family — such standards! — and as he paused to reach for his stein I thought I had earned the right to a few questions of my own. In a small alcove beyond where Maria sat, impatient to be off on our date, I could see propped against the wall a hurdy-gurdy of ancient manufacture.

"Oh, you collect grind organs, do you?" I drawled urbanely. "They're rather amusing, I think. A marvelous nostalgic quality quite unlike anything else, don't you agree?"

Mr. Italia laughed heartily at this, slapping a thigh encased in trousers tight as sausage skins. "That's a good a wan! As though I gotta time for hobby. You think I gotta time for licka stamps or sticka coins in book after I cranka she all day?"

Again the leap of getaway joy inside me, a vision of things other than those that obtained. Oh, definitely! I saw the tall polished doors through which a houseman carried cocktails on a tray difficult to set down amid the books littering this house of impeccable taste, where I would be such a frequent caller. But how much there was to escape from first! Two families suddenly instead of one. I cast an anxious glance at Maria, for we had been indiscreet. What a horror if . . .

"Where do you keep the monkey?" I asked, resigned to the worst.

"Down a the base. The janitor he's a let me keep Jenny in the furnace room. Monkeys need to keep warm, you know — tropical animal. Jenny's old now, I need another. But" — he sighed — "cost too much a da mon'." It was now Mr. Italia's turn to scrutinize his daughter, thinking in hope what I had in terror. Well, I would not take her off his hands! "Cost too much a da mon'," I thought rather crudely to myself as Maria and I set off for the park.

"I'm like you, Don," she said, laying her fragrant head on my shoulder as she took my arm in her two hands. "We both want to get away from home."

"Why is the awfulness of families such a popular reason for starting another?"

"Well, that's a mute question."

It was clear that Maria and the other neighborhood girls I dated would have constituted an escape into a provincialism worse than that whose bonds I longed to break. They failed the selective principle now already so profoundly at work in me that there was scarcely a moment of reflection on the future but provoked some image illustrating this idea of worldliness. Girls like Maria did not measure up to my standards. Neither did I, but I would. Provided I steered clear of entanglements that might arrest, perhaps forever, my development in that direction.

Fantasies of what might happen if I did not filled my mind by way of stern warning. I would stand before the windows of the numerous borax furniture stores that dotted the neighborhood and stare at the "parlor suits" and "kitchen onsombles" there, immersed in the most abysmal depressions as I evoked, from the patterns of tritely set tables and chairs, whole married lifetimes of banality. Some of my slightly older friends were already buying such furniture, in preparation for such lives. These glimpses were like visions of hell, of an intellectual and spiritual perdition into whose attendant quagmires of E-Z credit terms and twenty-years-to-pay I must at all costs avoid putting my foot. I decided to break off with Maria at once.

"Don't you want to do the right thing?" she asked.

"I can't."

"Why not?"

"Religious reasons. Our faith doesn't allow us to intermarry."

"But you say you're rebelling against all that."

"It would still kill my mother. And, Maria, it wouldn't be fair to ask you to wait as long as you'd have to. I want to go to the University next year if there's money."

We sat on a park bench, in observance of her wish that we shun the seclusion of the foliage till we had "come to an understanding." She was a very nearly beautiful girl, grave, never silly like so many of her contemporaries, smiling oftener than she laughed. She was far from frivolous, her sexual freedom being the expression of a warm and spontaneous nature, not of any quality to be identified as "fun-loving" or "fast." The familiar figure of O'Malley the cop went by, his stick dancing on its thong; then we had to move back from each other for an approaching couple. "Let's go in here where we can talk," I said hoarsely, drawing her toward the shadow of the bushes. Visions of the borax furniture stores vanished as she followed with little more than a sigh of protest. We sat down on my spread-out trench coat in a narrow clearing between the shrubbery and the railroad embankment. My conduct was not a calculated abuse of her favors but a surrender to temptation like her own, for I did not believe for a minute her story that I had been her first lover, though she was mine. She spoke of her father and his willingness to let us use the parlor provided we came to this "understanding." "It's your body to do with as you please," I said, forcing her back down against a murmur of protests. When she sat up again abruptly, I knew that she was terrified at something glimpsed over my shoulder.

Through the branches parted with a rustle shone a large star, above which could be dimly discerned the moonface of O'Malley the cop, screwed into an expression of official perturbation. "What's goin' on here, my Oi ask?" As we scrambled to our feet he added, with a humor no doubt perfected by long practice in these circumstances, "Or maybe Oi should ask what's comin' off here?"

We made out the case that we had sought the privacy of the shadows merely to pet. That itself was forbidden, however, in the quarters selected, giving rise to the fear that we would have to be run in to the precinct station and booked on a morals charge. We turned sick with fear. In a voice without timbre, I poured out a torrent of entreaties, begging O'Malley to think not of us but our parents. "It would kill my mother," I said.

"And my father will kill me," said Maria. She wrung her hands and sobbed wildly. A few bystanders had collected on the walk beside the open grass on which the scene was enacted. "It's because he's so strict that we have to come here at all. Let us go, and I swear on the name of my dead mother that we'll never come back here again."

Whether because his own Irish heart was plucked by this maternal reference or because the wish to play a role more magisterial than that of pounding the gravel was momentarily gratified, O'Malley relented. He pointed his night stick at us as we fled toward the gates of the park, a youthful Adam and Eve banned from a municipal Paradise by one of the lesser and more colloquial angels at heaven's disposal. "Oi'm lettin' you off with a warning this toim, but remember, next toim it's booked ye'll be."

The number and variety of accents and brogues to which I was early subjected seems notable now, though they were not untypical of that part and that period of Chicago. Beyond the horizons of our Dutch household — whose speech was Americanized at best into "dese" and "dem" and "de bot' of us" — lay the vast crazy quilt of other European-born elements composing the Eighteenth Ward, in which we lived. Even today, after more than a quarter century of exposure to more cultivated societies, correct English still rings a trifle strangely on my ears, while the perfection of the educated Londoner is downright freakish — the ultimate in the foreigner.

The problem with Maria was one the shattering episode in the park helped resolve. We never went back there again, and since neither the porch nor the parlor at Italia's conduced to intimacy, our relationship became less and less one about which any "understanding" had to be reached, or our spirits racked. Too, a wedge of shame — like that of Adam and Eve — had been permanently driven between us. We had a few more dates at the movies (where the guardians of the morals were ushers playing flashlight beams among the entwined couples), and then Maria took up with a boy who seemed more "serious." We had forgotten each other by the time I started life at the University, on money earned during the summer delivering telephone books and selling vacuum cleaners door to door, supplemented by what my father was able, rather more generously than had recently been hoped, to contribute. He had sold his ice route and gone into a far more lucrative line of work. It was, in fact, the business in which the better social element among our folk, at least the financially more snobbish, had amassed their means — garbage hauling.

four

I T WAS NOT until my sophomore year that I achieved any foothold in the purlieus of sophisticated America, and by that time I had had a direct dose of my family's new economic status, which stiffened my will to a degree that can be imagined. Summers, as well as Saturdays during the academic term, I had to help my father on the sanitation truck. It was while doing so that an incident occurred of the sort that are of no external consequence but serve to illustrate some private incandescence of spirit — in my case, this hankering for the fleshpots of Egypt.

Our collections were of course commercial — restaurants and grocery stores with refuse in excess of what the city would take — and lay mostly in the fashionable Hyde Park district, now more than ever connotative of elegance for including the University Midway. The very names of the places we serviced — Coq d'Or, Luigi's, the Balalaika — struck my heart with the resonance of gongs. How often I would pause in the kitchens in the act of removing barrels and tubs, to gaze a moment at those farther doors beyond which, at dusk, the scenes would unfold of which I dreamed in endless apotheoses: urbane men and women chatting across the crystal and linen of well-set tables, each of which was an island in a sea of glamour. Of that cavalier world I had no doubt I would in due course be a charmed participant.

It can be imagined, therefore, with what resentment I approached my first barrel of swill. Handling such barrels and, especially, heaving them up the sides of the truck required a skill not easily mastered, and any aesthetic resistance to the task made it for a beginner doubly arduous and even dangerous. There were then no conveyers into which the container could be tipped at convenient tail-gate height; it had to be swung up so that its middle landed precisely on top of the truck, as on a fulcrum, from which the contents could then be tilted out. Any mistiming could result in disasters of varying gravities: throw the can too far and it would itself land in the truck and have to be fished out, not far enough and it might slide out of control and empty itself in the alley or on oneself. More than once the apprentice in this case miscalculated, to find himself covered with coffee grounds and copiously festooned with fruit peels.

My main fear was that as we neared the campus I might be recognized. At least that was so in the beginning. I soon saw that nobody ever looks at a garbage man, with whatever consolation the truth had to offer. Besides, if one of my classmates did glance in my direction he would never recognize the figure in the clown's canvas gloves and pith helmet (worn as a safeguard against poor timing), and if he did he would not believe the testimony of his senses. Often it was toward noon that we approached the University, by which time food was uppermost in my mind. It was at midday, one Saturday in September, that the incident already alluded to took place.

The whistles had just blown for lunchtime, a ritual to be observed as far from the truck as possible. We had finished picking up at Luigi's, which had a garden behind, latticed off from surrounding courts and hung with Japanese lanterns, somewhat worn from a summer's use but still swaying brightly in the breeze. My father wandered out to the street in search of a tree under which to open his lunchbox, but I, after a quick look around to make sure I was not observed, slipped into the garden with mine. Luigi's was only open for dinner, so the garden was deserted and the tables not yet laid. I sat down and opened my lunchbox on the bare surface of one in the farthest corner.

As I munched my sandwich and sipped cold milk from my Thermos, I heard strains of piano music drifting across the backyards from a nearby house. I recognized one of Chopin's *Études*, executed with a merit I felt I could appreciate. I drew a certain pleasure from the speculation that I might be the only one within range of the music on whom its nuances were not lost. When I had finished eating, I stowed my lunchbox in the cabin of the truck and went for a walk around the block.

I passed my father snoozing under an elm, a bandanna over his face to discourage the flies, to which we were ever magnetic. I strolled on. I had made one right turn and then another when the sound of the piano became once more audible. It struck me suddenly, like a spray of sound, infinitely sweet on the summer air. It flowed

43

from a red-brick Georgian house furred with ivy, its chaste design relieved by a burst of baroque over the doorway, where twin scrolls crowned a broken white pediment like a pair of swan's wings beating valiantly in the cause of Romance. To this visual note the music seemed an answering echo from some pining ally, invisible yet near at hand. The beauty of it all, together with the mounting sense of myself as its keenest triumph — a commentary on our time — induced a kind of intoxication that made me recklessly steal up to the open window from which the music issued, where, partially screened from the street by a row of firs, I looked cautiously into the house.

The room I saw was a tastefully assembled opulence of red velour chairs and landscapes framed in gilt, of Sèvres vases and damask draperies — between tasseled scallops of which I gingerly peered. The pianist was a spruce blond man of middle age with a clipped mustache, in a white linen jacket but no necktie. He sat with his back partly to me, his hands bouncing lightly off the keys in the manner of effortless virtuosos everywhere. Repetition of a single passage suggested a composition at which he had not quite attained a perfection suitable to himself. I presently saw that I was not his sole audience. A woman his own age sat in a silk dressing gown, listening with a frown that at first seemed a display of cross spirits but soon revealed itself as expressing critical concentration. When he finished, the woman looked over at him and nodded grave approval of a sort that conveyed more praise than a burst of applause would have done. The man rose and on his way to her picked up a box of matches in order to light a cigarette she had shaken from a pack. After performing this office, he blew out the match and then kissed the tip of her nose before walking out of the room altogether.

But this was precisely the sort of thing I wanted to do! As an illustration of worldly style the profounder for its negligent air, the scene could hardly have been improved upon. It thrilled me to my roots. I do not wish to labor this point about worldliness, but it is almost necessary to do so in order to present it on a scale at all commensurate with its importance to the yokel gaping at the casement ledge. Worldliness to a reared Calvinist is not a vague entity but a specifiable sin of a higher order. The privilege of predestination, of being one of the Elect, carried with it the command to "come out from among them and be separate." It is only in the light of my long incarceration within that principle under conditions of immigrant inferiority that my drive to reverse the order and get out there and be one of them can be at all understood. A special pleasure adhered to the name on the mailbox of the house into which I was rubbering — Van Allstyne. This meant that the people were Dutch, so my profane relish of their mode entailed no disloyalty to the racial, but only the religious, half of my heritage. They were surrogates, my proxies in the ways of wickedness until I could be groomed for their assumption myself.

But pauses in the day's occupation were not always so exquisite. Late one afternoon, I saw my father leave the alley behind a bar and grill we serviced called the Hi Hat (the kind of "swank" place springing up everywhere since the repeal of Prohibition) and head down a gangway to the front door. "Where are you going?" I called.

"Let's get a sandwich. I'm parched."

Now my father could never get it through his head that the establishments from which we removed refuse were not the same as those to which he had once delivered ice. They had been *saloons*, in which the iceman was not only allowed but expected to plunk down a pinch of his profits at the bar with his own sort; these were *cocktail lounges*, frequented by people of the kind among whom I planned to find my portion later. He seemed to see no difference, but would sail into the latter as though he were welcome as the flowers in May, though emitting an air which cleared a generous path on either hand and assured him his choice of stools at the bar at any rate.

"Plumber and his helper," he ordered in the Hi Hat, into which I had followed him out of curiosity no less than thirst. It was a snuggery a step or two below street level, with a buttoned-leather interior reflected in a dusk of blue mirrors. In these could be also dimly discerned a cluster of white-collar onlookers far more curious than I, who now wished I hadn't come.

"A what?" the bartender asked.

"Plumber and his helper. Shot and a bottle of beer. A boilermaker. And give the kid a Coke," my father said, ordering no food whatsoever.

The next five minutes were something to be got through. I drank my Coca-Cola with my head down, aware of faces wreathed in smiles. These people could slum for a moment on their home ground, how amusing! Hateful people, of whom I would soon be one! Let them wait and see.

"Ain'tcha got no Heineken's?" my father asked when given a bottle of domestic lager, and I longed to sink

46

through the floor. I gulped down half my drink and stumbled out, hearing my father turn democratically to a woman in a cashmere coat and inquire the name of the pink liquid she was sipping. In the security of the truck I sat burning with shame till he reappeared. He sauntered blithely into the alley, wiping his mouth with the back of his hand, unaware that he had broken every taboo in the social scale.

Driving to the dump, he chuckled at the memory of the incident and shook his head. "Those people with their fancy drinks. Didn't even know what a boilermaker was. Never heard of it." He laughed without malice but rather a good-natured superiority, the reverse of my own view of those café folk as constituting a touchstone of which I must not fall short.

My father's spirits mounted as we neared the dump. The road took a long, swooping dip under a railroad viaduct down which he always loved to gather speed for the ascent beyond, pulling on the whistle cord as we flew. The whistle operated on the engine exhaust, emitting a series of ear-splitting blasts that cleared the way far better than a conventional horn. "Hold 'er, Newt, she's a-rearin'!" my father shouted, as we sailed into the underpass. His face was lit with a smile rendered slightly maniacal by a missing front tooth — a foreshadowing of that derangement which, little though we dreamed it then, was soon to engulf him in actual fact. My mortification had worn off and I was glad to see him happy. His being the reverse of all I planned to cultivate in myself did not prevent my liking him. His elation, no doubt a more primitive version of my own at the Van Allstyne window, suggested the wild diversity of human make-ups.

"She's a headin' for the stables, Newt!" I chimed ecstatically in, remembering the Chopin. Next came a trolley line, and I felt a thrill of pleasure at the pedestrians gaping from the sidewalks as we tore across the intersection, the truck wide open and the whistle shrieking like mad, and then at the sight of our reflection in the store windows with the name Mid-City Cartage streaming in retrograde, above the slogan I had opposed in vain: Sanitary Sanitation.

We reached the dump at dusk. It was a mile or so of intermittently smoldering flats and pits along a highway near the city limits. It took no more than a touch of the poet to see in the palls of smoke and sluggish fires a dismally burning hell. I saw it as that region of the shades in which wandered forever the spirits of those who had in life buried their talents and thus been less than they might: the sin of stewardship. The gulls and other scavenging birds were harpies, wheeling over the noxious wastes while silhouetted against the colder fires of the western sky.

It was a winter sunset, and we were early. None of the other trucks regularly converging here at evening to deposit their loads had yet arrived. "Let's drop this one and get," my father said, slamming off the highway with the same high spirits that he had shown all the way over. He swung the truck to the left, stopped, and backed with a jerk into the section where we were dumping those days. His gusto worried me. We were filling a pit from which gravel had once in the past been mined, and if the hazards of maneuvering on fairly open ground were bad enough, those of backing toward a precipice of swill will need no elucidating.

"Easy," I said, when he banged to a stop on the exact brink. I was outside the cabin now, guiding him back. "You're right on the edge, Pa. Put the emergency on!"

"Hold 'er, Newt!" he called from the wheel in the mood of our recent exchange.

"Be sure the brake is on before you dump now."

He pulled up the emergency and then threw the lever that tilted the body and sent the day's accumulation sliding out.

The drop was not sheer where we were, the crater being more saucer- than cup-shaped, as well as by now nearly filled, but that far from eliminated the need for prudence. I watched anxiously till the truck was empty, and, once back on the front seat, felt a sense of relief when my father shifted into gear and shot forward as soon as the body had settled. We went only a foot or two and stopped. We felt the left rear wheel sink. "Damn," my father said, stepping on the gas pedal. Accelerating only made the wheel spin more futilely, and presently it slued over till the right wheel was in the same trouble. I have spoken of the brink of the pit as though that were clearly definable, but actually it blurred into surrounding ground itself obscured under numerous disposals. It was in these marshy approaches that we were apparently foundering. They could be treacherous as a ditch of snow. My father began to rock the truck as one does in snow, shifting rapidly back and forth between reverse and first, to no avail. There was no traction.

"Look," I said, genuinely alarmed now, "let's just wait for someone to pull us out. Put the brake on and leave her. There'll be a truck along in a minute."

But my father was temperamentally incapable of just

sitting and waiting. It was this trait that was responsible for the course matters now rapidly took. He sat for a minute or two with the motor running, and seeing no sign of a fresh arrival, began rocking again in search of a patch of solid ground. The rear wheels only sank deeper into their ruts. Then suddenly the incessant back-and-forth motion underwent a change: we went back without going forward. Inch by inch the truck slithered down till the front wheels were also off high ground, the nose of the engine hood tipping at the same time ominously skyward. The list of the truck, which had been careening slowly on my father's side, steepened abruptly, and garbage began coming in the window like water through the porthole of a sinking ship.

"Jump!"

This was advice on which I had begun to act before I heard it. My door in its now nearly horizontal position constituted a trap door which had to be flung upward. I opened it and leaped out, my father so close behind me that he landed on top of me, flinging us both to our hands and knees in filth. That seemed to have no bottom here, which was about a dozen feet from "shore" as one instinctively thought of it, at a point where the pit began to fall away rather steeply. The rule might have been supposed the same as that for quicksand, not to struggle, but one didn't think of that. In our panic we scrambled and thrashed our way toward safety until, suddenly hitting a pocket more liquid than solid, we sank to our chests. In later years I was to read of a play which Samuel Beckett, the author of *Waiting for Godot*, promised his public, the sole action of which was to consist in philosophical exchanges between two characters buried to their chins in garbage cans. This was precisely the condition in which the following colloquy took place, save for the principals' being engulfed in a valley of abomination rather than individual containers of it.

"Think we'll make it?"

"Have to hold still, Pa. Wait till help comes."

"I will lift up mine eyes unto the hills, from whence cometh my help," my father quoted in a dramatic change of heart, at the same time scanning the horizon for trucks. We were at a distance below ground level at which only the tops of vehicles were visible to us, and these only dimly in the failing light. "He will save Israel, and that right early."

"Feel around for something solid. But easy."

We both did so, worming a foot at a time in a gingerly radius around us. We banked for salvation on the large amounts of scrap metal often mixed among the more perishable matter. Presently my father did touch something firm, a large box or crate, onto which he cautiously stepped. He was suddenly clear above his knees. After an exclamation of pious gratitude, he reached a hand toward me. "I think she'll hold both of us. Easy now, boy," he said, as I waded inch by inch across the six feet or so that separated us. I never got to him. Halfway there, my own foot encountered an obstruction, and I found myself standing on something metallic and flat, perhaps the side of a perambulator, or a bed-end. Thus we both had adequate support from which to witness what happened next.

We had had to call to one another (and my father to the Lord) above the noise of the truck, the engine of which had all this time continued to run. Now it stopped, asphyxiated by refuse, and rolled over on its back. An overturned motor vehicle is an unnerving sight, in some ways more so than a demolished one. Its exposed wheels and underside make it resemble some monstrous but helpless beast, and it is this "helplessness," paradoxically, that gives it for the moment the look of something other than mechanical. Our truck lay in this position for only a few seconds. Then it began to roll and tumble down the slope in the avalanche it had itself unloosed. The horror of this was followed instantly by a worse. The box on which my father stood was sucked away in the landslide — or perhaps I should say garbageslide — and he disappeared from view, singing the doxology.

I stood on my own precarious pedestal aghast. "Pa!" I called, at the same time remaining carefully motionless lest even the physical exertion of speech dislodge my support and send me pitching in his wake. The truck had come to a stop some thirty feet below, on its side. Somewhere between me and it was my father. Vague local agitations suggested from time to time his whereabouts, and once I thought I saw a hand waving above the wastes, in salutation or farewell. I was about to call again when I heard a truck pull in, and frantically sent my shouts and gesticulations in that direction. Neither my cries nor my signals meant anything since the occupants of the truck could neither hear nor see me. But they were backing toward us. As I shot another look back into the pit, my father suddenly rose into view a dozen feet away, the song of praise again on his lips, and wearing, like a beret, one half a cantaloupe rind. I gestured toward deliverance, and we both stood motionless watching the rim of the pit. The helper got out to guide the driver back. He saw us, goggled at the sight, and hurried back to the truck for a rope. Within two minutes an end had been thrown to us, and we were being hauled to safety.

The truck was another matter. Cartage crews always carried ropes and chains to get themselves and one another out of trouble, but one truck could never have pulled another out of that hole, obviously. My father spent the next days phoning excavation and construction companies with cranes and other power equipment, but the estimates for the salvage job he described were so frightful that he dropped this line of thinking and explored that of regarding the truck as lost, to see if the "extended coverage" on his fire insurance policy didn't take care of it. It didn't. A panic worse than that in the pit itself overcame him. He paced the house with his hands in his hair; he rolled his eyes to heaven — though protesting, once again, that no kind Providence dwelt there.

Now occurred one of those grotesque ironies that are too strong for the delicate stomach of Art but in which reality abounds, as though life itself enjoys laughing down the aesthetic proprieties. Yet the resolution it brought was so obvious and simple that we all felt foolish for not having anticipated it. The dump fires themselves in their random course at last reached the truck; a well-oiled engine and a full gasoline tank assured a speedy incineration. One look from the edge of the abyss by the claim investigator, and my father as good as had his check — for full recovery.

He lost no time in buying another truck, on which he had already set his eye. It was a Mack, sturdier and more up-to-date than its predecessor, of course glitteringly new. It was during my Christmas vacation that he got it, and I went along on the maiden voyage. My father was in the soundest spirits I could remember; the world once more made sense, and as for God, he moved in a mysterious way, etc. For a Christmas present he gave me a tendollar bill to buy some books I wanted. As for *Moeke*, nothing was too good. After our last call on Christmas Eve, he drew to a stop in front of a drugstore with an exceptionally fancy display of toiletries in the window.

"What are you stopping here for?" I asked.

"Get Ma a bottle of perfume. Not just anything, but the best, so come on and help me pick it out. I think she'd like perfume. She's been dropping hints about that lately."

It was with these changes in my background that I took my first step into the world known within that background as, simply, "American people."

Archie Winkler was a member of my sophomore class who took me home for a drink one afternoon following some whispered aid I had given him in a biology quiz. His house was near the University and not far from the Van Allstynes'; a houseman in a white jacket opened the door for us as Archie searched his pockets for his key. The butler was slight and towheaded like Archie, who introduced him as Hewitt. That could have been his first name, such was the familiarity between them. We proceeded into the drawing room as a trio rather than a pair being ushered there by a servant, gaining its cavernous glories by way of a short flight of stairs over whose carpeted treads I dragged my toes in order to polish my shoes, of whose condition I had become at the last moment mindful.

"Your mother keeps giving me this fudge about fifty not being too many for the party," Hewitt said, sauntering between us with his hands in his pockets.

"She'll have to go," murmured Archie, reading some mail he had acquired in the hall.

This exchange gave me the feeling of breathing air very rare indeed, a sensation heightened by the Manet in whose shadow it was concluded. The canvas had that overly stunning, almost meretricious, quality of originals. The attention they call to themselves as such, to the oils laid on by a vanished hand, overcharge the aesthetic experience for the viewer, who oftener sees a fetish than a picture. It was what I saw in the Manet. Either way, it nearly threw the room out of balance, no mean feat among that quarter acre of Aubusson rugs, niched bronzes, and rosewood chairs upholstered in pink brocade.

"You like it? I picked it up in France two years ago," said a voice of such low register that I was surprised to see a woman at my elbow. She fastened her scrutiny upon the landscape a moment herself before transferring it to me, and saying, "I'm Mrs. Winkler," as Archie from a distant bar called my name into the proceedings.

Thus I had in the span of a few breaths encountered my first butler, my first original and my first globe-trotter — for the references to where she had acquired each object in the room of which she now took me on tour left no doubt of the scale on which Mrs. Winkler pursued her wanderings. You knew Mr. Winkler was dead; she had too much that air of fixed proprietorship that compensates widows left in plenty. Her Hebridean tweeds, Persian scarf, and Dresden teeth suggested one half of the couple seen smiling at ship's rail in the advertisements illustrating the sunset years of those who have invested wisely, the investor himself in this case having been scissored out of the picture and fallen overboard.

"Have you ever been abroad?" I was unexpectedly asked.

"No, but my parents have," I said. "They've spent many years in Europe." I remembered my father ill in steerage and my mother's rocks from the Zuider Zee — one of those winds from the heath of memory by which the Fates see to it that we pay as we go by being most miserable when most happy.

Archie bore down on us with Martinis, singing a song of which the words were both revolutionary and bawdy. His mother beamed. She approved of what he had brought home, thanks largely, I think, to her impression that my family were old New York Dutch, a delusion with which it seemed to me for the moment wisest not to tamper. She asked me whether I knew any of the Roosevelts. After we had chatted in this vein of old friends for a bit, she excused herself and vanished into the back reaches of the house, trailing the hope that I would come to the party they were giving on Saturday next. "Oh, he'll come, Mater," Archie said, speaking again from a remote corner of the room where he was now slouched over a telephone. He was busy inviting other friends of his, though having just agreed with Hewitt that the guest list was far too long already.

I sank into one of the chairs to savor my good fortune. I seemed to have struck my pick into a fine vein indeed.

"It's one of Mater's ghastly affairs," Archie was saying into the phone as he snicked away some ashes from a cigarette, "but the Dreisers are coming, and just possibly Fabian. Come and disintegrate with the group."

This was it! The urbane drawl, the prattled wit, the indifference to the answers at the other end — supplying just the right tincture of snobbishness — were the sort of thing one had had in mind. All I could see of Archie was his back as it shook with laughter over news of some companion given, it seemed, to pouring coffee on his Shredded Wheat, but that was practically all there ever was of Archie's mirth in the way of outward signs: nothing showed in his face, which expressed at best a wry amusement with the race of man.

He finished his calls and then we talked for an hour about schoolwork and related concerns. When I rose to go, he saw me to the door. There, as he opened it, he said in a lowered voice, "Look, could you let me have a ten or so till the first of the week? I'm a bit squeezed, and if Mater . . . I mean would you mind awfully?"

Mind, of course I didn't mind — then or a few days later when, his financial skies seeming not to have cleared in the interval, he touched me for another twenty. By that time I had tasted the lavish hospitality of the house in the form of the Saturday soirée, but there was more to my willingness than gratitude. It seemed perfectly part of the pattern for a rich American family to have a son who was a ne'er-do-well, or "rotter," up to his ears in gambling debts best concealed from his mother; it went with the stereotype.

When by the end of the school year, however, Archie had sponged close to two hundred smackers with no sign of reimbursement, my enchantment with the world of fashion began to slacken, and my feeling toward Archie palpably to sour. At that time my own family had tough sledding, due mainly to some newly arisen complaints of my father's calling for a procession of neurological specialists, each more baffled than the last, and so I decided to hit Archie for my money. At one of his mother's spring garden parties I took him aside and asked him point-blank when he was going to pay me back. He looked at me in surprise, as though there were some incongruity, even a breach of etiquette, in the spectacle of a guest dunning a host. Perhaps there was. But school term was over, and I had just resumed full-time work on the garbage truck, a fact which reminded me again of how hard-earned my money was. Something else had happened that set my back up. While driving along on the truck, I had seen Archie emerge from a restaurant at the head of a gay little group, flinging bills to menials bowing in his wake. This seemed to me to exceed the limits of permissible rottenness, and I vowed to see myself repaid by hook or by crook.

His mother — still calm in her faith that I hailed from Eastern elements so secure in their breeding that they could reverse custom and send their children West to school — invited me to her annual Fourth of July lawn party — over Archie's dead body, as he had become thoroughly disillusioned with me. I made a tight-lipped point of coming, knowing it would be my last chance to buttonhole him before the fall term — perhaps my last chance ever, for he had spoken of changing to Dartmouth, a threat which, as it turned out, he made good. Early in the evening I saw my chance, and strode across the grass to join him on a stone bench on which I found him momentarily alone. "Look," I said, "I need my money, and I need it now." Archie rose as one caught in mid-gesticulation at another guest, in this case a young girl named Nellie Winters who was sweeping toward us on a billow of tulle. After being introduced, I sought a clump of rhododendron behind which to collect my thoughts, and from whose protective foliage I could hear Archie tell the girl, "He's a wet smack."

Now this expression suddenly characterized the whole kit and caboodle here. I had since first being awed by them glimpsed enough of the Real Thing — tea at a professor's house, a drink with a classmate whose family supported the local symphony — to know that the Wink-lers were *ersatz*. One did not in circles of true quality hear terms like "wet smack"; they went with "Mater" and "swanky" and all the gimcrack rest. But we mount the ladder of sensibility rung by rung, passing through levels in which we use words like "swanky" and "brunch" before attaining those from which they will be seen as the semantic stigmata of a lower order, and unthinkable on our lips.

I remained in cover a moment to rally my forces and decide on a course of action. At the end of the drive I could see the off-duty policeman handling the parking problems always entailed by the Winklers' parties, proof again of their coarse prodigality. Sight of this cop did nothing to soothe my ruffled spirits, for I remembered seeing Archie on a previous such evening slip him something from the wallet I had helped stock. Seething among the shrubbery — from behind which my hand had plucked a drink from a passing tray, to the consternation of the waiter bearing it — I debated taking my grievance to Mater herself. I rejected that idea. Mrs. Winkler had once related having seen in her Caribbean travels a peasant flog a donkey with a rooster. Well, I would not flog the mother with the son. Not that she herself enjoyed anything like the prestige she once had in my eyes. Far from it. I now saw the vixen, even the dragon, lurking behind the Gracious Hostess. Consider, for instance, the dinner served that night.

A famous beauty in her day, Dolly Winkler still liked to gather around her specimens of her successors, whom, nevertheless, she resented and possibly even loathed for being still young. She loved to show up the new set as examples of diminishing *élan*, of a generation lacking the physical and sartorial style that had characterized her own. The menu that night might have been sadistically chosen as a sort of obstacle course over which the competition were challenged to show their poise, if any. First there was artichoke, a boiled whole for each, to be disassembled leaf by messy leaf, dipped in drawn butter, and dragged across the teeth. The debris of that removed, there came fried chicken and corn on the cob. What remained of composure vanished among the heads bowed over slathered ears and the sound of kernels exploding like shells in the summer air. Butter ran down the chins of women reaching for napkins by now themselves hazards to cleanliness. Still there was no respite. Dessert was watermelon — great wedges of it to be eaten by the damp beauties around whom, on the grass, lay scattered pips like the black seeds of Dolly Winkler's hate. It was the one time I heard guests ask for the bathroom as though they intended to bathe in it. All this while Dolly Winkler toyed with a little white meat and nibbled a grape or two from the centerpiece overflowing with fresh fruit.

It was no doubt from the black seeds of my own anger, well watered by cocktails, that the plan sprang which I now suddenly conceived for recovering the money due me. I would steal it back.

From the time or two Archie had invited me up to his room to wait with a drink while he took a shower, I knew where he kept his wallet. It usually lay on top of his bureau when he wasn't carrying it, and he wasn't carrying it now as far as I could judge from a hard look at his white linen jacket. I recalled his having had to dart into the house for it that night before paying the policeman. After dinner, my confidence in this project perhaps enlarged by the table wine I had taken aboard, I joined the file of guests repairing to the house in search of bathrooms, of which there was no dearth there. I went directly to the second floor, in the hallway of which I leaned negligently against the wall, like a man awaiting his chance at the chamber occupied by two women audibly laughing and splashing tap water. After making certain the floor was otherwise deserted, and hearing no newcomers trooping up the stairs, I went on tiptoe to the open doorway of Archie's room.

I knew the layout here perfectly. There was a lamp burning in the room, and the billfold was quite visible on top of the bureau. I should have preferred less illumination for my work, but then I suddenly thought of sauntering freely into the bedroom toward the bathroom adjoining it, as a guest accustomed to feeling at home here. It would be a perfect explanation were I to be seen going in or out. After another glance around to make sure no one was around, or coming, I walked up to the dresser, picked up the billfold and opened it. I was in luck. It was a goodly sheaf of currency that met my eye, some tens and at least one twenty I saw as I folded and thrust them into my pocket. Perhaps sixty or seventy dollars in all. That left a balance of well over a hundred dollars due me, which I should never see again unless I supplemented my theft with some valuables easily salable in a pawn shop. A wristwatch lay ticking on the bureau surface, and nearby was a gold cigarette case. Should I pocket them, Raffles-like, as a rough equivalent of the host's remaining obligation? Could one take something possibly having sentimental value even though one had a moral right to it? These questions raced through my mind as my heart pounded and my throat tightened. Hearing voices on the stairway again, I turned and shot toward the door. Standing in it, and blocking my passage, was nothing less than the figure of Hewitt.

"Yes, sir?"

"I thought Archie wouldn't mind my using his bathroom."

"What were you doing at the dresser?"

"Tidying up." My voice squeaked out this inanity as my head throbbed. It felt like a balloon about to burst.

"What is it?" Hewitt glanced down at my pocket, in which my hand still clutched the bills.

"I'm only stealing what's mine."

"Then you were."

"Look, Hewitt. This man owes me two huh — huh — huh — "

I wondered whether if I brushed past Hewitt the other

components in this fantasy would dissolve into thin air, and whether my legs would postpone their metamorphosis into rubber until I had managed to gain the street.

"What would you — I mean if you were in my . . . ?" The words trickled like a weak liquid down my throat. Hewitt turned to look toward the stairs, at the foot of which could be heard Archie himself in a gay banter with some guests.

"Archie!" he called.

"Yes?" Archie's head appeared at a turn of the landing.

"Would you come up here a moment, please?"

We stood rooted in our respective positions while Archie joined us, frowning inquiry. Hewitt waited until another pair of laughing women had locked themselves into the bathroom before saying: "Mr. Wanderhope was at your dresser. Perhaps you'd better take a look at your wallet."

My hand detained Archie.

"I took the liberty of helping myself to what you owed me — or the interest on it," I said, recovering my tongue at sight of the culprit who had driven me to such extremes. Archie laughed through his nose, shaking his head. Being a rotter, he at least refrained from holding others in moral scorn. Indeed, he seemed to derive a certain pleasure from another's venality, as narrowing the disadvantage against him.

"You really are a dose, aren't you, Wanderhope?"

"You're in a poor position to judge, I'd say."

"Shall I call the police, sir?" It was the first time I had heard Hewitt address his master with that vocative. Perhaps the occasion had rallied in him some dwindling vestiges of dignity. "There's one right outside, of course."

"The traffic cop. Yes."

"No," I bleated.

"Why not?" There was an impish gleam in Archie's eye; I felt that he was not so much toying with the idea of summoning the law as tormenting me with the threat of it.

"Would you want a scandal?" I said, with such a threatening tone as I could manage. "Because I'll drag everything out. How much you owe me, what a dead beat you are. Giving parties like this while other people have to . . . Medical bills . . . "

I had given Archie in the course of pleas for reimbursement an inkling of my family's cash picture, and it may have been the memory of this ingredient in the crisis, as well as my threat publicly to arraign his wastrel ways, that made him desist. A story in the morning *Tribune* about a gay Hyde Park party ending in a shabby night court altercation could not have been to his liking any more than to mine. He may have visualized me bolting through the crowd amid bromidic cries of "Stop thief!"

"Go on, beat it, Wanderhope," he said. "And don't ever show your face around here again."

"Don't worry."

As I made my way down the staircase, a fierce flare of rebellion — perhaps peasant rebellion — made me fling the last word over my shoulder. Pausing on the landing I called up: "I hope you've learned your lesson. You with all your — This neighborhood — One admires these houses, oh, sure. Till one has a chance to see what goes on in them!"

With that I went out, quickly but without panic. On

the sidewalk I turned sharply and, breaking into a trot, headed for the trolley I customarily took into this part of town. I made my usual transfer at Halsted Street, rode south to Seventy-third, and walked the three blocks to where I lived.

My mother was waiting for me in the window.

five

My FIRST ASSAULT on the strongholds of fashion had failed. But recognition of the fact implied no intention to capitulate or regard withdrawal as anything but temporary. Of that many-bastioned world I had scaled the wrong wall, that was all; a moment to lick my wounds, reconsider my target, and off once again.

Meanwhile an interval with a Dutch Reformed girl seemed in the making. Her name was Greta Wigbaldy, and she was a niece of my father's late partner. Blonde as the butter she would have been churning had her parents remained in the Netherlands, she stood sufficiently detached from our present background to see me as I saw myself, a sort of reverse Pilgrim trying to make some progress *away* from the City of God, and she was sexually spirited enough to require a word other than "seduction" for her share in the pleasures which (my taste for public parks being now sated) we took on the miles of beach that are Chicago's other civic feature. There were haunts where even as one kissed one was drunk with the classic shoreline: the tall apartments beneath whose windows these night waters broke, the Babylonian hotels with names like Windermere and Chatham whose lights inflated the heart. There was a necklace of moons strung on a strand called Michigan Boulevard, which swept northward through the Gold Coast and out to the suburbs of Evanston and Winnetka, where the last mansions waited.

"You're always a hundred miles away," Greta said one night. We had left the rocks and the parked cars with their embracing shadows and were walking along the beach, deserted except for one other couple we saw, their coat collars turned up like ours against the October cold. We passed a pier with its haunting sound of waters plashing among rotting piles, and came to a bathhouse, the knobs of one of whose doors I tried without success. We stood with our hands in our pockets before a peeling poster. It seemed a lithograph of two naked figures locked in a Priapic clasp, till scrutiny of its accompanying text revealed it to be an illustration of mouth-to-mouth resuscitation for a rescued swimmer.

Trudging back along the sand, we encountered two other members of our congregation, climbing down out of the high rocks and suggestively encumbered with blankets. They were Pearl Hoffman and Jack Dinkema. A shy attempt of Pearl's to avoid the meeting was shaken off by Jack, who drew his arm from her grasp and came over to greet us heartily — for reasons I could well understand. He had no automobile, and escorted his dates to these lovers' lanes by trolley. The ride back which he saw in me undoubtedly inspired the invitation, extended with great warmth, that we be his guests in a late snack. He knew an all-night bakery where you could get doughnuts so fresh they lay in an indigestible lump in your stomach till morning, so we all piled into my car and made for it.

The term "my car" is a misnomer too, for that matter. The Oldsmobile I drove was Wigbaldy's. Greta's father was a building contractor for whom things were going more than well, an expansive man typical of what we mean by Dutch *gemoedelijkheid,* and I had scruples about putting his generosity to ends of which he could scarcely have approved. But Greta overrode them, rather irritably. "What difference does it make how we get to where we're going? You don't have qualms about what we do in the parlor, do you? Well, it's his house the same as it is his car. Why is one abusing hospitality and not the other?" This was only one glimpse she gave me of the thoroughly practical morality of women in matters of "the heart," once they are committed. Another was the solution of this ever-vexing problem of rendezvous which she now proposed. It took my breath away, like her love-making.

Wigbaldy had begun by erecting single houses, mostly bungalows, on vacant street lots. Now he had acquired backing for a twenty-acre development of thirty or so medium-priced "homes" to be disposed with conscious rusticity among winding roads and named Green Knoll — though no relief of the flat terrain was apparent to justify this designation. The pilot house was up by early spring and was instantly furnished for display as a Model Home and thrown open for public inspection one Saturday morning. The day-long file of visitors brought out by advertisements in the real estate sections of newspapers augured well for the Green Knoll project. Wigbaldy celebrated by taking us all out to dinner, which ran late into the night, frustrating again the young lovers. Greta now put forth her mad proposal.

"We'll use the Model Home."

"Good God."

"I'm sick of beaches and rocks, and the parlor's no good either," she retorted, giving me, as she often had, the sense of discontent, or of emotional fret, rather than any real joy of life. Her buxom good looks were qualified by a certain sullenness about the mouth, the corners of which were often twisted down in that grimace so common among her sex. "Daddy remembers what he did on the dikes, but I wouldn't trust my mother not to snoop around after pretending to be asleep. It's nerve-racking. So is all this hemming and hawing. I want to go to bed with you."

"Greta, could we?"

"Why not? It's locked every night and there's not a soul in the development. Not even a watchman. And don't start about abusing hospitality — my father doesn't even own the house any more. It's been sold to some people who won't move in till summer. So I'm not going to let it go to waste. It's completely furnished, including the bedroom. The bed's made. It's even turned down."

Logistics no less than casuistry were among the arts in which I was now schooled. Greta managed to purloin a key from her father's study, of which she had a duplicate made, restoring the original to his desk. She bought a set of peppermint-striped sheets and pillow cases to match those on the bed in the Model Home, which would naturally have to be made again after use. I had no doubt that for as long as we might have occasion to alternate linen in this dream nest she would have fresh ready when we stole in.

We walked the mile or so from her house to the sub-division, some mention having been made of Wigbaldy's possible need for the Oldsmobile that evening. Not that I would have accepted it. While I was now fairly demoralized, as well as aflame with the prospect of an hour in his daughter's arms, the thought of using his car to debauch his bourgeois paradise was a perfidy at which I drew the line. I carried the sheets, of which I had been given custody, in a bundle said to be a package of books I was taking to a sick friend. We cast a last look along the inhabited street up which we had come before turning in the pillared gateway of Green Knoll, under a shingle reading "The American Dream," and striking up dark Willow Lane toward our lair.

We crept in by flashlight, extinguishing even that once we were safe within the harbor of the bedroom. We undressed in darkness, dropping our clothes on the floor in our haste to be together.

Greta's zest during that long-pined-for hour came as no surprise to one who had tasted it in less conducive circumstances. We lay peacefully enough for some time afterward. Not as long as we might have wished, though. The traffic on the far street had not disturbed us; they were but sounds of the rude world, sweetly invading our reverie. The noise of one car seemed to detach itself from the general hum, however, till it was clear that someone had turned into the subdivision.

"Just driving through," Greta murmured, shifting a ponderous thigh against mine. "They do it all the time."

The vehicle drew to a stop before the Model Home.

Some suspicion of the use Wigbaldy might have had for the Olds tonight began to dawn on me. The motor was shut off and, weak with horror, we recognized Mr. Wigbaldy's voice as he shepherded some clients up the stairs. Sounds of words and laughter mingled with the footsteps as a key was inserted in the lock.

"My God," Greta whispered. "What'll we do? Oh, my God . . . "

I could not manipulate my tongue into the variety of positions necessary for speech — not that I had any constructive suggestions to offer. We sat bolt upright, yet paralyzed. Then we popped to our feet and began to scramble about in the darkness for our individual clothing, only to have a light from a corridor switch send us back into bed, where under the covers, lying on our backs, we tried to wriggle into such garments as we had managed in the interval to snatch up — I into some underthing of Greta's, as it happened, and she into mine. In my panic I tried to keep clear a portion of my mind with which to evaluate the prospects; in particular, how much time we might have in which to make ourselves presentable. That depended on which of two available routes through the house Wigbaldy took his clients on. One was through the dinette and kitchen first, which would give us time to dress, possibly even escape. My knowledge of his tactics led me to fear that he would begin with the sleeping quarters so as to "climax" the tour with the electrically furnished kitchen so impressive to the ladies. A woman's voice in the imminent corridor saying "Look at this wallpaper, Art. Isn't it artistic?" confirmed this surmise. Apparently the visitors were to have their climax first.

They were now inches from the open door. With

what remnants of sanity remained to me, I speculated that surprise might be as disrupting to the intruders as to us, and that they might, after noting that the bed was occupied, be relied upon to beat a hasty retreat, leaving us some interval in which at least to dress. If we kept our faces concealed we might, God knew how, escape recognition. So I whispered "Lie still" to the still writhing Greta, and pulled the sheet over our heads.

I heard Mrs. Wigbaldy's voice. "Now this is the master bedroom here, Miz Walton," she said, feeling along the wall for the switch. "I want you to notice — "

A ghastly light broke over our heads as we pulled the sheet higher, wrapping it around our ears. We lay on our stomachs. A collective gasp came from the arrested party.

"Well, *God verdam* . . . " said Wigbaldy, after what is termed by writers of romantic fiction "a long moment." "*What is me dit?*"

He drew back the sheet, enough to answer the question. The discovery was dramatized by a cry from Mrs. Wigbaldy, who was no doubt aided in her identification of the bodies by the female clothes, familiar to her, strewn about the wall-to-wall carpeting. Greta herself was now emitting sharp little squeals of horror and protest which were muffled by the pillow in which she had buried her face. I reached around and jerked the sheet back over our heads. "Can't you go away, please?" I said. "We'll discuss it later."

I was aware of Mr. Wigbaldy shooing his prospects toward the kitchen, but Mrs. Wigbaldy came a step closer to the bed. She was a short broad woman, with an extremely wide middle narrowing steeply toward her shoulders, in shape not unlike a brandy snifter. She bent down and through the bed sheet shrieked into my ear the single word:

"Prude!"

This good woman, at best only half Americanized, had a number of such imprecise terms of which that example comes most readily to mind. She knew it only to be an epithet relating to conduct in matters of sex, and took it to mean a wanton indulgence therein, unable to imagine a system of values in which an opposite attitude could possibly be deemed a fault. She flung many another denunciation my way, curses cut short when Mr. Wigbaldy, having seen to the safe disposal of his guests, came back for what was now a hysterical wife. Hauled forcibly from the scene, she shouted that I was a skunk and a rat and a number of other things including "Slut!" and that she would have me for a son-in-law as speedily as the law permitted, and no nonsense about it.

Thus that specter was materializing which had of old haunted me as I had stood staring into the windows of borax furniture stores, with the added sting that the dinette and bedroom "suits" which had so oppressed my spirit must now be broadened to include the walls within which they stood. For there was presently — after somewhat more sober discussion with the rather more realistic Wigbaldy — talk of our taking one of the "homes" in Green Knoll, Greta and I, with the down payment as a wedding present. "From me and the missus," said Wigbaldy, with shattering good will.

The next week was a week in hell. There was no religious excuse for wronging the girl in this case since we were of the same faith or, what was even more to the point, lukewarm about the same faith. The horror was of

73

those dream houses and what they typified in the way of a progressively more standardized culture, which one assumed some rapport with on the part of the girl since her father built them. What one saw was fifty years of stupefaction flat as the plains of Illinois, with its boredom at mealtimes and children to perpetuate it all. Imagine my surprise then at the answer I heard when, sitting in the parked Oldsmobile in sight once again of breaking waves, I asked a question generated by prolonged view of the petulant profile.

"What's the matter, Greta? Don't you want to go through with it?"

"It's not that so much as living in one of those awful houses."

She sat forward, chin on fist, in the manner of The Thinker, while I waited in amazement for her to continue.

"I know you like luxury and security, Don, but . . ." The rest came out in a distraught gasp — "A *development!*"

"Darling, you mean — ?"

"I hate them! I'd rather live in a tent."

I writhed on the seat, raking my hair with joy. One had for months been so busy fumbling at clothing in plotted assignations that it hadn't occurred to one to make the acquaintance of the girl with whom one was thus enmeshed. Conspiracy had monopolized all our thoughts.

"You mean you hate those houses too, and those awful breakfast nooks?"

"The very word depresses me. I want a *house*. I'm not saying Evanston or Winnetka, necessarily, or even the North Side, but a house, for us to be *us* in. To . . ."

I scarcely heard. Fear of the closing snare had blinded me to everything but the snare itself, to the very soul of the maid with whom I struggled within it. It was one of those simple apocalypses that open one's eyes suddenly to the obvious. Instead of seeing oneself at one end of a table, alien to all in the room including its other occupant, one saw himself and his wife linked in a companionate amusement with everything in sight — and, yes, a good deal of what lay beyond the windows. How we would ridicule it all! What fun we would have deriding the world, until something better came along.

"Well, I mean if you hate those houses that much too, why, hell, let's get married and move into one as soon as possible," I said, taking her hand. "We've got to make a start somewhere, some way, and that seems easiest at the moment. I mean financially and all. I'm not proud. And it isn't as though we had to stay in the damned thing the rest of our lives, is it?"

She sat huddled over herself a moment, and spoke, when she did, with a characteristic moodiness.

"I even dread marriage itself, to tell you the truth."

I moved closer and put an arm around her. "Darling, Greta. I never dreamed we had so much in common."

SIX

THE DISCOVERY of a bond with Greta other than physical set up within me a partial willingness to marry without completely stilling my anxieties about entering into that state. The resulting turmoil might be likened to that produced by those electric food mixers with two whisks geared to revolve in opposite directions. My mind was like a bowl of batter being simultaneously churned in contradictory ways by such a mechanism. Until, at length, the more recent of my excitements subsided, the relief of finding my apprehensions qualified wore off, and the apprehension alone remained — as though one set of blades had ceased to rotate, leaving a single agitation. Dread became again uppermost and, cursing my luck and myself, I wondered how I could possibly extricate myself from such a muddle. It was then that deliverance came from an unexpected quarter. Perhaps not totally unexpected, since it involved a factor in my life of which I have already given due account: my health.

Late hours and, as they said then, "dissipation" had weakened a constitution none too sturdy to begin with.

In the damp months of late spring I developed a cough, accompanied by a feeling of the most leaden fatigue. The condition persisted long enough for me to seek the services of that dubious healer and old friend, Doc Berkenbosch.

"It's not brownchitis," he announced one evening when he had called me into his office to communicate the findings from an X ray he had advised, "but it's the lungs." He cleared his throat noisily, as though scraping the words together from the depths of his own chest cavity. "Just the one actually, and only the apex — meaning it's only barely started and very minor. There, that make you feel better? *Och ja,* boy, the Lord gives us these things to bear. 'Ours not to reason why, ours but to do and — ' " He broke off, rejecting the rhyme toward which he had inadvertently stumbled, and began to throw some mail into a wastebasket as a means of bolstering my confidence. "And He gives us, thank God, the means of detecting them in time. Take my word this is nothing, it could be a blessing. Give you a warning to slow down. Take a little rest."

"How long?" I asked, striving to conceal the pleasure aroused in me by this diagnosis.

Doc shrugged. "These things can't be predicted. Year maybe. Maybe eight months, maybe eighteen. Now, now."

I had risen and walked to the window, where I stood gazing out at the tarred roofs and jutting chimneys the better to mask my emotions, as well as to gain a moment in which to ponder my good fortune. Doc came over and laid a hand on my shoulder.

"Don't be bitter."

"No."

"Because your hemogoblin ain't half bad, meaning your general condition can be counted on to help you throw it off. These little tubercles, I believe they call them, first show up on the apex. The fact you've got only one such spot on only one apex means — Come here."

He drew me to a wall on which the X ray was clipped to an illuminated panel, and pointed to a spot which I could scarcely distinguish from its surrounding shadows.

"Here you have the bronchi, at the point where they empty into the diatribe. There's the lung legion — a very slight legion, as those things go, take my word for it. Rest, plenty of fresh air, and you'll be as good as new in a year or less. Climate is a help too. Look, why don't you pack up and head out to Colorado for a bit? Our church has a crackerjack sanitarium out there, you know."

"Colorado!"

"Now, now."

The prospect of putting a thousand miles between myself and the Wigbaldys contributed greatly to the courage with which I was able to face my "blow" — a spectacle of grace and spirit which all who came under its spell found inspiring, a lesson worth taking to heart. This certainly included the Wigbaldys themselves, to whom I broke the news *en famille*, so as to spare Greta and myself the pains of private disclosure. Our numbers did blunt the moment's edge by somewhat diffusing the consternation that greeted my announcement, made with a certain gallant nonchalance.

"So it seems, you see, the old bellows are nipped. Nothing much, but it means putting oneself in dry dock for a bit, if you know what I mean."

78

"How long?"

"That you never can tell. Sometimes those things go on for years. Not that one is really ever the . . . So under the circumstances I don't feel I have the right to expect Greta to . . . " I said, coughing discreetly.

"There, there, now, Mrs. Wigbaldy."

"I called you a whore. That was wrong."

"It's no matter. We'll just forget the whole thing."

I was not the only one for whom the cloud had a silver lining. Even greater unexpected dividends were yielded my queer and complicated father, whose faith was finally bolstered and stabilized in the following manner.

Now the church was running a hospital for its own, not a charitable institution for every Tom, Dick, and Harry with tuberculosis; thus the qualifications of any claimant to the fabulously low rate of six dollars a week for members in good standing, as against more than triple that for nonmembers, were rigidly passed on. Since my father was the bill-payer in this case, it was his affiliation with the church that was duly reviewed — and found to be anything but shipshape. In fact he was up for excommunication, following a renaissance of his Doubt stimulated by a reading of the atheistic pamphlets of Robert Ingersoll. The last thing he had flung out to the delegation of elders come to labor with him in a last-ditch warning had been, "Don't bother to fire me — I quit!" This made him eligible for the steep fee, rather than the nominal, unless there was a sudden and radical change of heart. Evidence of this was presently forthcoming.

A tribal scene occurred more charged with hysteria, if possible, than that precipitated by Louie's announcement of the nature and contents of my aunt's belly. Pa tortured his bandanna and downed many a whiskey at a table thumped by his brother Jake, who said, "You see what you get for doubting God's word? Terrible expense!"

"Which we'll all have to chip in and help," cried Jake's wife, a woman ever torn between self-interest and family loyalty. "Poor as we are ourselves."

"We go all to the poorhouse," my mother moaned, wringing her hands.

From between cool sheets I heard the distant sound of tumult, shifting to a minor key as castigation gave way to remonstrance, swelling once more to a note of triumph as my father made his historic decision for Christ. A hymn was sung, "Bringing in the Sheaves"; then they all trooped into my bedroom to relate with beaming faces that Satan's grip on my father had at last been broken. Another sinner had been bound to the divine will through adversity (mine, as it happened, but that was a technicality). Pa was going to the consistory tomorrow night to affirm his reversal of heart, soundness of doctrine, and gratitude to God for salvation from a fate worse than death. Testimonials to this effect were heard now from the principal, after which they all dropped to their knees to pray. "Don't you want to join us?" Uncle Jake asked me, his face reflecting escape from the hell by which, as his wife had intimated, they too had been fleetingly singed. I replied that being flat on my back I was in a position more prostrate than theirs and could pray as well in it.

This over, I raised a hand in sign of weariness. I had no wish to break up the religious revival going on at the foot of my bed, nor the social life there either, but I had been ordered to get plenty of rest, and rest I intended to get in preparation for the arduous journey ahead of me. I softened these words with a little joke. "Now nobody will have to cough anything up except me," I said, smiling wanly. Oh, how they laughed and hugged and very nearly appreciated me! They were all on hand to see me off on the Burlington Zephyr, on which I arrived in Denver the next day, refreshed in spirit from the hours of gently rocking solitude. A pick-up truck from the sanitarium whisked me and my luggage out past the city limits to the hospital, where, having been ushered into the admitting office, I heard the institutional door clang shut behind me and saw an orderly appear. "This way," he said, taking my grips, and led the way into the back regions from which he had come.

It was then, for the first time, that the suspicion struck me that I might be sick.

seven

THIS WAS A FEAR fostered in no small measure by
the scope of the care to which I was now subjected. I was
steered into the infirmary by a middle-aged nurse and put
to bed with orders to remain there. I was given a thermometer, known affectionately here as a "temp stick,"
and a chart on which to record four readings a day (early
morning, noon, late afternoon, and evening) as well as
my pulse on each of these occasions. The nurse left, to
return with receptacles for specimens of more things
than need be named, but one of which, blood, was
drawn from a vein while I gazed negligently at the trees
outside my window. "Your meals will be brought in. The
doctor will see you sometime tomorrow or the next day
or the next." And so on. "Meanwhile, I repeat, stay in
bed."

Thus were banished my visions of a sanitarium as a
place where one sat on benches philosophizing in the
sun, in the manner of *The Magic Mountain*, or contracted
imprudent passions in the music room. I raised myself
on one elbow and gazed out the window. Beyond a row

of evergreens stretched a length of flagstone walk on which presently two codgers materialized conversing wildly, shaking their heads and with that maximum of gesture familiar to me as the pantomime of theological dispute. I dropped back on the pillow, emitting a long, baleful moan.

Adhering to the ceiling, I now noted, were inspirational thoughts slanted to the shut-in. They were not the hospital's idea of interior decorating, I learned later, but the work of a previous inmate whose principle had been that, to the bedridden, the ceiling bore the same relation that walls do to those privileged to live perpendicularly; therefore "wall mottoes" belonged properly overhead where their contents could be absorbed in prostration. These truths were pasted to the calcimine. Most were from the Gospels and St. Paul and therefore possessed literary merit, but a few appeared to be creations of the muralist's own, being crudely inked on squares of what seemed to be shirt cardboard. One such effort read: "Flat on your back? Best way to see Heaven." Another: "Maybe this will make you upright in heart."

I rolled over from supine to prone, half expecting to find similar maxims affixed to the floor, for moments of true despair. I thought moodily of home, of the University, of Greta. . . . Rolling up an eye, I took inventory of the bedside table. On a linen tidy were a Bible, the temp stick, and a small clock reading five-fifteen. Enthusiastically, I sat up and poked the thermometer into my mouth. Time for the afternoon reading.

I improved the five minutes I had been instructed to leave the thermometer under my tongue by gazing out at the distant Rockies, seen today for the first time. I tried to guess which might be the celebrated peaks among those mantled with perpetual snow. One seemed to have a cross of white upon its side. The original of the Longfellow poem? "There is a mountain in the distant West that, sun-defying in its deep ravines, displays a cross of snow upon its side. Such is the cross I wear upon my breast these something years . . . something something changeless since the day she died." As I tried to reconstruct the verse, and to analyze the failure of the range to flood my being with aesthetic awe, the door was kicked open by a young nurse with a face like an amiable sparrow who entered with my supper.

"Well!" she said with that humoring air reserved for children and invalids. "Seeing the sights?" She set the tray down on the table and heaved her shoulders with a bright sigh.

"Yes," I mumbled, removing the thermometer. "Now, which is Mount McKinley?"

"That is in Alaska. You mean Pikes Peak." She leaned across the bed and pointed through the window. "There it is — the tallest one."

I jerked her into bed, tore the clothes from her back, and raped her, in spirit. When she had gone I consulted the thermometer, noting that my brow had become beaded with moisture as a result of these exertions. The mercury stood at ninety-eight point six. Normal. Avidly I made my first entry on the chart provided.

After supper, I read a chapter or two of Ecclesiastes, then listened to a bedside radio equipped with earphones. My temperature at eight o'clock was the same. I fell into a deep sleep, from which I awoke with the certainty that I had been unconscious only an hour or two.

The room was still dark, but I sensed some compulsion to look out the window. Above the gloom still over-spreading the earth, the snowpeaks were a flaming scarlet in the first rays of the rising sun.

The middle-aged nurse appeared in the course of the morning to say that the doctor would see me at eleven o'clock; meanwhile, I might sit for a few minutes in the easy chair and read the morning *News*, which she had brought me.

I had the end room of this wing in the infirmary, so there was a single window at right angles to the main bay exposure next my bed. The sun was streaming through this window, and swinging the chair around, I sat in its rays stripped to the waist, the chintz curtains parted and the sash up. As I basked in the luscious warmth, the door opened again, following a short rap. An elderly man's face was thrust into the room, wearing an expression of tentative cordiality which quickly froze into a violent frown.

"Are you mad!" he said, rushing into the room and drawing the shade. "Who gave you permission to sit in the sun and with your chest exposed like that?"

"Why, nobody, I . . . It felt so good to — "

"To be alive? Well if you want to stay that way, keep out of the sun until you're given permission. Worst thing in the world for most T.B. patients — can stir up trouble, reopen old lesions."

"I'm sorry. I naturally thought the sun — "

"Common mistake. You don't take it unless it's spe-cifically prescribed. Is that clear? I'll examine you this morning, and then we'll see whether you join the Sun-shine Club. I'm Dr. Simpson."

He held out a hand of which the skin was loose as a glove, and which remained extended while we both despaired of my getting my own through my tangled pajama-sleeve in order that I might grasp it. He had a salt-and-pepper suit so natty, linen so fresh, and shoes so polished one read into them instinctively a meticulous and no doubt vain nature. An ironic smile encircled teeth too white to be his own, a smile echoed in deep-set brown eyes capable of all the forms of mockery, one felt, save self-mockery. He asked whether this was my first taste of the West, and hurried off before I could answer, as though the impressions of sight-seers were inherently tedious.

It was a half hour later that I shuffled in pajamas and robe down the corridor to his office, which lay between the infirmary and the ambulatory wing. By that time I had learned that he was an old lunger in his own right, possessed Scotch Presbyterian origins, and preferred making the jokes himself.

He was standing at the desk when I entered his consulting room, his head bent over a cardiogram. Fingering untidy festoons of this, he resembled a stockbroker surprised at the ticker tape. He finished his scrutiny of it before dropping it on the desk with a cryptic smile.

His examination was brief. After an X ray by a woman assistant, he fluoroscoped me and then listened to my chest, instructing me first to cough into my fist and then to repeat "ninety-nine" monotonously as the bell of the stethoscope stalked my ribs. He dropped the stethoscope on the desk and told me I might get back into my pajamas.

"Well, I can hear a little music in there, but I don't

think it's playing 'Nearer, My God, to Thee.' Just the very tip of one side has any *râles* whatever. Very little activity. Next to nothing."

"How long — ?"

He arrested me with a hand. "Give me a chance to ask you not to ask that question." He made a brief, no doubt set speech, to the effect that the longer he practiced the less confidently he could predict when anybody would go home, if ever; that he had seen people enter these gates with no very noticeable lesions six years ago who were still on hand, while others with craters you could have dropped billiard balls into left in as many months; that added to all the honored ministrations of rest, food, and fresh air was an imponderable which he would simply call mental attitude. He had evidently drunk deep of the newly welling springs of psychosomatic medicine. "I used to think mental attitude half the battle, then seventy-five per cent of the cure; now I'm not sure it isn't more like ninety-five. Or maybe I should say ninety-eight six." The ironic grin conveyed the malicious implication not to be stated: that if one determined the prolongation of a disease, mightn't one also have willed its acquisition? "I have more people in here than I can tell you, about whom I wonder what they're running away from. You will no doubt make a game of picking them out for yourself."

"I wasn't going to ask when I could go home," I lied. "Just when can I go to ambulo?"

"You pick up the slang fast." He waved an indifferent hand. "Any time. Why don't you give the infirmary another week, then I think we'll have room for you in the ambulatory wing. There's a man moving out of there back to the infirmary," he added, with that sardonic gleam in his eye which was not to be confused with a mischievous twinkle.

As he rose and shook my hand, I could not resist another question.

"Not many go *back* there, do they? I mean Eugene O'Neill overcame it, and Gide, and didn't Maugham once — ?"

"Ah, yes. We have some of those too, as you'll find when you hear the typewriters starting up in ambulo." He looked at me in alarm. "You haven't brought one, have you?" I assured him he need have no fears on that score. "Good. Then why don't you come to dinner at the house soon. Mrs. Simpson and I occasionally have people in on Thursday evenings, and we're always especially glad to find someone who won't read us the first act of something. In fact we collect discoveries — Young Men Who Don't Write. You're mine, remember. I saw you first."

Thus that circle of kindred spirits for which I had pined, that urbanity that I had loved long since and lost a while, was to be found right here where I had least expected it — in the bosom, however infected, of the church. What I had thought to take by storm fell into my hands as simply as fruit from a tree.

On hand when I arrived at the good doctor's house, a half-timbered Normandy cottage just inside the sanitarium gate, were most of the regulars currently composing the band of Elect whom the Simpsons — themselves apparently put to it for society in this eventless backwater — cultivated and maintained for their "Thursdays." They all looked up from their chairs in speculation, even alarm, when I entered, a scrawny youth in a tweed coat which fit him too soon, in a torn pocket of which he clutched a cold pipe by no means to be lit under the doctor's eye, a prospect definitely on probation. Mrs. Simpson, a plump, effusive woman the reverse of her husband, propelled me amiably before her for the round of introductions.

First was a portly native of Amsterdam named Carl Horswissel, who wore a Norfolk jacket and a string tie. I had seen him from my window promenading the grounds. He spoke with a thick Dutch accent and was said to be a ruined cocoa importer. The most formidably intellectual of the lot was Leslie Foyle, a Colorado mining heir whose family could well afford the fees exacted of Episcopalians. A clear-cut snob, his air of aloof languor was naturally aided by a pulmonary condition noted officially as "third stage, moderately advanced." The blue nails in which his drooping fingers terminated recalled to mind the old term "phthisic." Next were a voluble couple who were not patients at the sanitarium but neighbors of the Simpsons. Their name was Twitty, and I was surprised to learn they had domestic discord, which they freely aired. In fact, long stretches of these Thursdays were devoted to the ventilation of their problems, on the complexity of which they tended to preen themselves. They had tried to save their marriage by bicycling through the Palatinate, and it was to a travelogue of a spring so spent that much of this evening was given over. For the immediate moment, however, it was I who was subjected to note, rather like a fraternity prospect of whom as yet precious little is known.

"Wanderhope here has so little wrong with him," Dr. Simpson began in his most derisive vein as he poured me a sherry, "that he's practically an impostor. I could hardly detect any *râles* at all. So I'm going to try out a pet theory of mine on him. Short doses of really awful exercise, to see if winding the patient has any curative powers. All this sitting in bed blowing up balloons!"

"Yes, really, Horswissel," Foyle interjected, "don't you realize it's all a mammillary obsession?" Horswissel, without having the faintest idea what had been said, nevertheless wriggled with pleasure at being the butt of so erudite a thrust. I learned later that he had squeaked into the Elect by the skin of his teeth, and that some among them openly considered his inclusion a mistake.

"There must be a better way of exercising the lungs. Maybe deliberately getting the patient out of breath is it," said the doctor, handing me my sherry. "We're breaking fresh ground for you."

"Already?" I bleated humorously.

This was best absorbed by the final member of the group, a chubby youth named Bontekoe who aspired to be its clown. Most of his contributions were puns, following each of which he would raise an arm to ward off an expected blow, at the same time sinking down in his chair in a display of guilt. He was from Detroit, and in his "sophomore" year here. He and Foyle were among those suspected of having abused the Simpsons' hospitality by reading aloud selections from their works. Bontekoe observed now that Dr. Simpson had so many "pet theories" that he ought perhaps to set up shop as a veterinarian, and shrank into the depths of his wingback.

In sharpest possible contrast to my social life with this band of the Elect, by whom I was tolerated at least on approval, was the roommate with whom I was paired in ambulo.

He was a Kansas primitive named Hank Hoos. His hulking six and a half feet suggested an allegorical embodiment of Rustic Manhood to which the sculptor, perhaps due to an untimely death or loss of interest in the subject, had not put the finishing touches. His rough-hewn good looks were crowned by waves of glossy brown hair which he spent hours at the dresser combing, sagging at the knees in order to keep his head in the glass. It was hard to think of Hoos as ailing, and he dealt a damaging blow to Dr. Simpson's theories of self-invalidation since he had obviously only one thing on his mind: to get out of there and resume the womanizing this incarceration had interrupted. He had now done eight months of his "stretch," as he called it, and gave warning that he could endure little more unless his sexual needs were met — criminally if no other means soon presented themselves. Before I had quite unpacked my things he asked me if I had any information as to whether saltpeter or any other antiaphrodisiac was put in the food. When I professed ignorance of this whole matter, he asked me to pledge myself to get to the bottom of it with him. Walking across the room to put a few shirts into a drawer, I murmured some evasive reply, not clear in my mind whether he considered such dietetic resorts desirable or to be opposed under conditions thus delineated as taxing. Outside on the porch where we slept, our beds standing foot to foot, he spent hours relating some of the amorous exploits he intended to revive. Then one night, after bouncing into position under the covers, he suddenly said: "O.K., now let's hear about you. When was the last time you were with a girl?"

This was all too easily recalled, of course. I told him about Greta and her family, withholding names to protect the innocent, as he had certainly not done in the case of his cornland friends.

"Her father was a real estate contractor," I narrated softly in the dark, for only frame partitions separated the porches and I could hear Horswissel breathing alertly twelve inches from my head. His Montaigne had already been heard in its nightly drop to the floor, like a third shoe. "We were so in love," I said, wincing at the clichés by means of which I strove to gear my odyssey to my audience's comprehension, and at the same time divorce myself in spirit from its rather shabby content, "but had a hard time getting together. We felt we had our right to happiness. Then do you know what happened? Her father put up a development with a Model Home in it. We went into that one night. It was completely furnished, hey."

"You went to bed?"

"You know it."

"Tell me everything that happened. Don't leave out a thing."

It was a point he need not have pressed. In my eagerness to oblige, like those club members making "frank" revelations of amorous details not all of which have occurred, I thought I had an insight into the motives and techniques of the so-called "honest realists" of literature — honest to the point of mendacity.

"Her father was fit to be tied," I whispered when I reached the part having to do with our discovery. "He nearly killed me before he was hauled off bodily by two men. His wife stood there screaming bloody murder — a hysterical madwoman. She tried to bash my head in with the vanity stool," I improvised. "But it was worth it. Ah, that hour before we were busted in on," I said, hoping by such untypical descents in speech to invent a character who was "not myself," to whom could be attributed the admittedly sordid lapse of which I was being guilty.

"Tell me everything about it," Hoos said. "What was she like?"

"Now see here."

"What difference does it make? I'll never see her. What kind of breasts did she have?"

Talking about Greta in this fashion was simply out of the question, but feeling I owed Hoos some return for the tales with which he had regaled me — my own share in the game we were after all playing — I rhapsodized in terms applicable to womanly beauty in general, those visions and fantasies by which, indeed, we were scarcely for a day untormented. "Think of lilies," I said, "of lilies in mounds of drifted snow . . . " Hoos flung an arm over his eyes, as though shielding them from some blinding light or intolerable pain. At the same time Horswissel's bed creaked sharply and was still, as the man no doubt got on all fours with his ear to the partition.

I broke off, ashamed of myself. But I had already begun to see myself as Hoos saw himself, a prisoner of inflammations that time and improving health could only intensify. Perhaps T.B. had been a mistake. There must be a better way of evading reality. It was with matters at such a pass that I made the third connection of what I recall as a sort of triangular life during those fall and winter months at the sanitarium.

In the dining room, which was common but segregated, I saw one evening a new face on the women's side. A slender girl with blonde hair gathered into a ponytail sat gazing downward as she waited for the bowls of food to reach her. She listened to the chatter of the women among whose hands they passed down the table, smiling when appropriate, but keeping her eyes fixed on her blank plate. Her hands were folded in her lap, and she had a habit of chewing the insides of her cheeks. I inquired about her from Horswissel, who was on my right. He said she must be the girl just moved over to ambulo from the infirmary, where she had been for a year or more. She had had a pneumothorax, the operation by which gas is pumped into the pleural cavity in order to collapse the lung on one side. She was said to be shy and rather religious. In her pale face were the roses obligingly supplied by the disease to either cheek. Her fair hair prepared me for blue eyes when she turned once toward the men's tables — perhaps sensing she was being watched — but what met mine was a soft fawn's gaze of the most melting brown. Something shot along the surface of my heart like ice cracking on a pond. Her head bowed momentarily lower, lifting the gold tassel of hair off her neck.

I scarcely knew what I ate. I hurried to the main lounge after dinner, arriving just in time to see her walk up the corridor to the women's wing with a rather formidable maiden lady of middle age who was notorious, even with the chaplain, for the hymn sings she organized

94

in her room when other people wanted to read or rest. I loitered on the gravel path outside the women's porches, hearing there presently a swell of feminine voices coming clear and wonderfully sweet through an open window:

> There is a fountain filled with blood
> Drawn from Immanuel's veins,
> And sinners plunged beneath that flood
> Lose all their guilty stains.

I returned to my room feeling melancholy and vaguely troubled. The mood continued all through the following morning, Sunday. I failed to see the girl at breakfast, and made no more progress except to learn that her name was Rena Baker. She turned up at midday dinner, after which she was again swept from my view in a tide of companions making for the women's ward. I did not mind this frustration too much, having by now devised a plan. I went to chapel that afternoon with a will.

The sanitarium chaplain was a charming codger of great sensitivity and learning whose pithy sermons were anything but a bore. Today, however, we drew a substitute, a visiting parson so long-winded that his mid-service invocation carried us well past the point at which old Wenzel would have released us into the summer sunshine. Early in its course I stole a glance over my shoulder at Dr. Simpson. He had the look of a man dozing rather than praying; the familiar smile curled his lips, as though some irony too fine for consciousness were turning on the lathe of slumber. Knowing Rena to be sitting directly behind him, I gave my neck another quarter turn. Her head, under a solemn bonnet, was bowed. It lifted just then, and the eyes opened — and banged shut again.

After the benediction I hurried out as fast as the lagging congregation would permit. From the chapel steps I saw her walking toward the main building, alone. I overtook her on the gravel path.

"How did you like the sermon?"

She brought black-gloved palms together in surprise and laughed — a whispered little laugh that conveyed a feeling of the most intense reserve yet the most curious intimacy. "Well, anybody who talks for forty-five minutes on the value of silent meditation . . . "

I fell in beside her as we discussed the minister's text, which had been the words from First Kings in which Elijah finds God not in the wind nor the earthquake nor the fire, but in the still voice. We agreed we had heard too many sermons on this verse, which was supposedly calculated to disarm prolonged and complex exposition. By now we had reached the sanitarium. Sounds of tea being poured in the main lounge reached us on the doorstep where we lingered.

"Will you have some with me?"

She again joined her palms, stiffening her fingers as though to tighten the fit of her gloves. "Oh," she cried in that rippling whisper of a laugh, "I'm supposed to chase till supper." This was institutional slang for resting — chasing the germs. "I'm here on trial, you know, and I don't want to go back there." She pointed in a loop over my head to the infirmary. "Some other time though, maybe."

"My name is Don Wanderhope. I already know yours."

It was three days later that I found her alone again.

She was sitting in the lounge reading some mail, including a religious periodical of which she clutched the crumpled wrapper in one hand. "Oh, it's you again."

"Perseverance of the saints. How about a walk? It's nice and bright."

"Well, a short one. I'll get my coat."

Thus began a relationship which I pursued with a kindled heart and what are known as honorable intentions, but one subject to a tarnish for which I had only myself to blame. I mean its natural misinterpretation by the one-dimensional Hoos.

This lout's gossip of our observed ambles about the grounds and into the surrounding fields at first annoyed, then infuriated me. I entered the men's lounge one evening after seeing Rena home, as it were, to hear the conversation come to a stop so sudden there could be no mistaking its theme. A patient changed the subject with a gusto obvious enough to banish any remaining doubt. This was a recent arrival named Niebuhr, a professor of economics from a Midwestern college, here for his second stay. Niebuhr could rarely be got off his professional ground once he had secured the floor, and would discourse on real wages and gold reserves with a heat that was needless since no one there understood what he was saying enough to take issue with it even were he so minded. But he would harangue away till some impassioned declaration would explode in a fit of coughing, the results of which he would commit to a small *crachoir* carried on the person for that purpose. An economist with conspicuous consumption was all Bontekoe needed to make his day, as he soon let us know, ducking behind an arm to fend off the expected cuffs.

I sensed a certain constraint in Hoos's manner when we went to our room after the bell and set about preparing for bed. He retired without a word. The next evening I hurried out after dinner to keep a tryst with Rena behind the garage, into which we sometimes slipped to sit in the pickup truck and talk in peace, I behind the wheel, she with her head on my shoulder. We must have resembled a pair of young lovers going for a drive, or rather rehearsing for the glad day when they might do so, in a vehicle of a more romantic sort, of course. As I went down the corridor I caught faint footsteps behind me and turned in time to see Hoos dart into the lounge, with a last-second effort at nonchalance that was something to behold. The next time it was he who went out first, to stalk me from God knew what cover, for I was now certain that he was spying on me — or on us. The mystery deepened when he vanished on an evening when I stayed in, and stole back into the room in stocking feet long after Lights Out. Asked where he had been, he was at first evasive, then blurted out, "I'm stir-crazy. I warn you." He flung the words at me accusingly, as though I were in some way responsible for his plight.

The huggermugger reached its climax one night when I had no date but slipped out for the purpose of decoying Hoos into the open in hopes of getting to the bottom of this thing. This much accomplished, as was discernible from the stealthy padding in my wake, I strolled past a clump of firs where, screened from his view, I suddenly doubled back and raced around the sanitarium water tower in a wide arc that fetched me up in arrears of my pursuer. He presented rightly the appearance of a dog who has lost the scent, but my relish of his bafflement was short-lived. No doubt assuming I had vanished for my rendezvous in the garage, he stood looking through its soiled windowpanes, shading his eyes, then went around to the back and listened at the closed door, again resembling a snuffling hound. So he had indeed been spying there. And not alone there, I presently learned.

I went for a tramp about the grounds, to cool down and calm my nerves. As time for the Lights Out bell drew near, I made a last swing around the women's wing, in hopes of catching a glimpse of Rena for a moment out-doors — or even a snatch of evensong — but was arrested instead by a figure of another sort. It was Hoos again, peering surreptitiously over the porch rail into Rena's room.

I slipped into the shadows when he turned his head, instinctively avoiding embarrassment. I was squatting in cover when the bell sounded and, presently, the rooms darkened one by one, suggesting well enough what had rewarded his gaze. I floundered in doubt as to what course to take. I was seething, yet loath to make mat-ters any more deplorable by creating a scene, certainly then and there. Watching a voyeur would appear a spe-cialty admitting of only one refinement, and our little nocturne had that. Hearing a rustle behind me, I turned and saw a pair of bespectacled eyes peering at me through the bushes. It would have been futile for Horswissel and me to pretend we had not recognized one another, and so, parting the breast-high foliage, I swam through green-ery to his side. "Shh," I said, leading him away by the arm. "Were you observed?"

"So dot's it. You got a good ting of it, watching de

99

girls," he said, as he permitted himself to be drawn onto the gravel path.

"Oh, this is ridiculous," I said. "For heaven's sake, man, let me handle this. Is that clear? Not a word of it must be breathed."

"No!"

It turned out to be impossible in the confusion to avoid Hoos, who, frightened off by noises, possibly our own, turned and bolted through the landscaping into our arms. The three of us now engaged in furious whispers, rendered more chaotic by Horswissel's lewd misconstruction of my plea for secrecy — his thought being to keep "a good thing of it" among ourselves — as well as by our being illegally abroad, so that we stole to the darkened men's quarters like a trio of desperadoes. Once alone with Hoos in our room, however, I lost no time in expressing my disgust with his conduct.

"Look, I'm no prig, but if you're going to do that sort of thing, I'll thank you to do it at somebody else's window. And keep away from the garage."

"It's all well and good for you to talk," he retorted, "but how do you think I feel, thinking of you doing pushups in the back of that pickup truck?"

"Now look, you bastard. If you've managed to see anything at all, which I doubt, you must know we just sit in the cabin."

"Don't give me that. And why apologize? Who wouldn't want to get out of this clink once in a while and cut himself a piece of cake?"

"If you don't shut your foul mouth, I'll shut it for you!"

"You mean this is the real thing?"

"Oh, you wouldn't understand."

"So you're smitten. Damned if he isn't smitten."

After this wretched colloquy, conducted while stumbling about in the dark undressing, I lay seething in bed for an hour or more. Could I gracefully request a change of roommate? The only double room currently half vacant that I knew of was Horswissel's, transfer to whose company could scarcely be considered an improvement. Despite his former money and pretense at reading the books that had gotten him by the skin of his teeth into the Elect, Horswissel remained for me a Dumb Dutchman whom I wanted to kick in the pork. And on sober reflection the next morning the whole idea of a move seemed ill-advised. Natures as coarse as Hoos's are often equivalently sensitive, and a slight could transform him from a nuisance into an enemy, possibly a very nasty one. It was all very well for Foyle to keep him at a distance by deliberate rudeness, as he said he did, on the ground that vinegar repelled more flies than honey, but his problem was not my problem. There was one ray of hope. Hoos had lately expressed confidence of being "sprung" after his next quarterly examination, a mere month off. Better to rub along till then.

Thoughts of Hoos's welfare, however, even for that matter my own, were banished from my mind by a turn in Rena's.

Her health had been precarious for some time. Now after an encouraging spell of normal temperatures she suddenly shot a fever of a hundred and one. She was seized by coughing fits that left her weak and dizzy, and were marked by increasingly ominous flecks of red. The doctor confined her to bed, which was a woe for me as well as for her. Men were barred from the women's dormitory except for the regular visiting hours, and my calls on her then were almost unfailingly ruined by the presence of other visitors or, what was worse, that of her roommate, Cora Nyhoff.

This woman loved God and hated men in nearly equal measure. She would stick around whenever I came, allegedly to help "cheer Rena up" but in effect to queer my progress with Rena, sensed as a threat to her own domination of the girl, of which I glimpsed an unhealthy side. The two had been paired off as being both "religious," stupidly, since there was no resemblance between Cora's bigotry and Rena's piety. Though Rena never admitted it, I suspected that the older woman had begun to pall. Indeed, I wondered if her continuous abrasive presence wasn't responsible for Rena's reversal. I was about to suggest as much to Dr. Simpson when I learned that she had gone back to the infirmary.

Here I could visit her freely with at least an even chance of not running into Cora when I walked in. Though confined to bed, Rena would sit on it tailorwise, drinking the tea I brought in or fingering the letters, papers, and books with which the counterpane was everlastingly strewn. She never held her teacup by the ear, preferring to warm her hands around the china, always watching me as she sipped, as though I bore constant reappraisal. We talked of poets, composers, the West, last Sunday's sermon — always last Sunday's sermon, of which a vital interest in human faith prompted her to be critical, as distinguished from Cora's dull evangelical chatter about "blessings." Divine worship was piped in for infirmary patients to hear from earphones plugged into bedside sockets.

"He seemed to think," said Rena one Sunday evening of a seminary student who had preached at vespers on the injunction not to cast one's pearls before swine, "that Jesus meant the pearls would only be ignored, but the text says clearly enough 'lest they turn again and rend you.' It's a popular mistake, but imagine a divinity student making it!"

"You could remove your earphones. I had to sit there and take it."

"Are you an atheist?"

"Not a very devout one," I reassured her, smiling from my chair. "I'm backsliding fast."

"Do you believe in a God?"

"With nothing certain, anything is possible."

"You're slippery as an eel, aren't you? Do you believe you have a soul?"

"No, but I believe you do."

With a terrier-like interest in everything that caught her eye or took her fancy, she would change the subject without a moment's notice. She now glimpsed, through the window, the figure of a middle-aged patient named Swigart, the sole Methodist among us, walking along with a cigar in his mouth. His affliction lay elsewhere than in his lungs. Rena reported that Swigart, a tobacco addict fated to have been born into a denomination where nicotine was proscribed, was happy for the first time in his life among the Dutch, who of course smoke like chimneys. "He's been declared arrested but won't go home," she laughed. "There's a story that he used to smoke behind the barn after he was forty, but it's probably too good to be true." We watched the object of this gossip, puffing contentedly, disappear in a blue cloud among the frozen lilacs.

"Do you pray for me?"

"Well, that would mean the one I was addressing had done this to you to begin with, which I find hard to believe anybody would."

"I don't quite follow you."

"I simply mean that asking Him to cure you — or me, or anybody — implies a personal being who arbitrarily does us this dirt. The prayer then is a plea to have a heart. To knock it off. I find the thought repulsive. I prefer thinking we're the victims of chance to dignifying any such force with the name of Providence."

"We're supposed to deserve it," she said, poking about in a box of cookies which my mother had baked and sent me, and which I had passed along to Rena.

"Not you."

"I'm a sinner."

"Stop giving yourself airs. You're beginning to sound like Cora."

"What would you do if you were God?"

"Put a stop to all this theology."

I came over to the bed and rummaged among the cookies too. Touching her hand, I took it and raised it to my lips.

"If we could only kiss," she said, pressing my fingers to her cheek. Under her silk pajamas I saw a neat, tilted breast, which I longed to touch. I started to sit on the bed, but footsteps in the corridor sent me ignominiously back to my chair. Munching a star-shaped cookie, I sat listening to Cora's voice greeting a nurse outside the door. Dull rage riled my emotion as I watched Rena, averting her eyes, tidy herself and the bed. I not only rose when the smiling visitor entered, but gave her my seat. I left instantly, as always seemed best under these circumstances.

But we had a beautiful afternoon the next week.

At dusk, Rena and I happened both to be gazing out the window when snow began suddenly to fall and the world to turn white under our eyes. Great feathery flakes descended in the windless air, weaving a veil of absolute white. Everything lost its outline. The mountains vanished; trees and houses were swallowed in a featureless void in which we watched mesmerized, not breathing a word. The room darkened slowly, and the monochrome outside took on here and there a golden glow as lights blossomed in every window but this. We hung suspended in a trance, an eternity of leisure. But mystic as the spell might have been said to be, it released desires long held in check. There could have been no errors now. When I drew near she averted her mouth with the gentle, rather rueful, movement with which she had always confined my kisses to her cheek, but my hand now grazed for the first time below her throat. I thought for a moment that encountering her own meant rebuke, till I felt her fingers at work undoing the buttons of her pajama blouse for me. Lying down, she offered up two small breasts as white as the snow. Bent to those, I heard her moan my name on the pillow. Beneath my journeying hand her slim body arched in a convulsion about which there could be no mistake.

"I won't ask whether I'm a virgin any longer after that."

"You know I love you."

"Isn't it wonderful? And we won't say anything about how insane it is."

"Everything else seems insane now. Except this."

"Yes. Oh, my God, here comes the supper cart."

Two days later, when I called, the room was empty. The bed had been stripped. Curtains blew at the open window. I found the superintending nurse at the linen closet at the end of the corridor. I imagined she had watched me emerge, then turned busily back to her work. She did not, at any rate, choose to withdraw her head from among the towels and linen while she answered my questions.

"Where's Rena Baker?"

"Not back from surgery yet."

"Surgery? What for?"

"Some ribs removed."

This was the last resort for patients whom pneumothorax and other measures had failed: collapse of the lung. She had not told me any such thing had been scheduled, or even contemplated. Nor that she had had rheumatic fever as a child and that her heart was not all it might be. I learned it all from Cora Nyhoff, to whom I hurried in the hope of more information than the bare facts related by the nurse.

I could eat no dinner. Rather ironically, the dining-room matron called on me for grace, which I managed like everyone else from a common store of clichés. Then I hurried to the infirmary. Rena was not yet back from surgery. I bundled myself into boots and overcoat and went outside. Rena's room was dark. Through the hospital windows, behind the infirmary, nothing could be seen but an occasional white apparition floating between the gaps in the draperies.

Tightening my scarf, I trooped around the sanitarium grounds with my gloved hands in my pockets. It was brutally cold, the snow hard as iron underfoot. The stars throbbed in the clear air. Jigging in the driveway ruts, I sorted out the constellations as taught me by Rena on our night walks; she was a country girl who had supplied my city-bred ignorance of the heavens, so that I could mark their mythological progress from my porch bed on wakeful nights. Orion, Cassiopeia . . . There were no Christians in that pagan congress. All the voyeurs were inside tonight. Some could be seen at their snug windows, watching. I went inside myself. After half an hour of hovering over a chess game in the lounge, and a few minutes in my room, I got into my clothes again and went out. As I neared the hospital, a courier came out and stumbled across the snow to the doctor's cottage. Dr. Simpson stood a moment in his doorway with the light behind him, nodding, then shaking his head. Then the caller left, and the doctor went back inside, not to reappear. The rooms in the dormitories darkened one by one. I hadn't heard the bell. Too late to make it now anyway. I walked to keep warm, wandering to the doctor's cottage, then back to the hospital. I stood irresolutely at the back door, raised my arm to press the bell, and dropped it again as my courage failed me. I went back toward the cottage, aimlessly. A bird suddenly rose from the brush beside the brook behind me, flew into the trees, and was silent. Another sound drew my gaze toward the gate. Under its arch a black vehicle rolled across the frozen snow, stopped behind the hospital, and a scavenger in a Homburg entered it carrying a wicker basket.

The stars swam in a mist of tears. The Rockies were invisible now, but I knew from memory where the mountain stood with the cross of snow upon its side. There was a cry from an animal down in the brush beside the icy brook, where nature was also keeping itself in balance. "Thou shalt not kill." This was advertised as the law of someone who had also created a universe in which one thing ate another. Were not believers aware of the holes a single thought tore in their fabric? Perfect love did not quite cast out fear, but rage did grief, or nearly so.

I walked around to the other side, where the wheels grinding in departure could be heard but not seen. She was as dead as the moon, who had warmed me. The little creeks of blood were stilled, the breasts I had kissed as cold as stone.

Dr. Simpson was evidently a watcher too, or someone had reported a delinquent by phone, because his door burst open and footsteps crunched the snow behind me. He had thrown on a coat, and his face above an untidy loop of scarf was demented with anger.

"What the devil are you doing out here?"

"Letting the moon open old lesions."

"Oh, for God's sake! What kind of tenth-rate Rossetti . . . ? Go to bed this instant! I order it! It's an hour past Lights Out. What the devil do you think this is, a country club?"

"I'm sorry, Dr. Simpson."

He came a step closer, scrutinizing me. "What's the matter with you?"

"Rena's dead, isn't she?"

"She slipped away quietly. The doctor in charge of surgery assured me." He hesitated, glaring toward the cottage. "Come inside. We'll both freeze out here."

The living room was empty. He kicked the remains of a fire into life and poured us brandies.

"Her heart gave out. Unexpectedly, because we checked it thoroughly, knowing she had a history of rheumatic fever. You can never tell about the heart — makes a fool of good cardiograms and bad. I have found women's as capricious as the poets say. Ah well, it may be a mercy, because frankly she didn't stand a chance. I doubt whether the collapse would have helped. It might have been a nasty third act."

"I admire the objectivity of science," I said, pacing helplessly about the room. "How they can — I had a brother once . . . Surely you no longer think this is a managed universe?"

"Why do you think you have anything to tell me, young man? I had a son once, whom I had to watch die of leukemia. He was seven. Stevie. He was such a boy as you see riding dolphins in the fountains in the parks. A dolphin boy. A faun. I watched him bleed to death."

"What did you do then, sing 'Come Thou fount of every blessing, tune my heart to sing Thy praise'?"

"Go on. I am an old man. I have shed my tears. Go ahead."

He went over to the fireplace and kicked the embers again. Then he walked to the window, where he sent a kind of snort between the damask draperies into the black night. He padded back to his chair, into which he flopped once more. I saw that he was wearing house slippers.

"The thing I must say is a little hard on me now is the operatic type we occasionally get here. All this *Liebestod,* and going off into the night and one thing and another. I had a romantic a few years ago who went out for walks bareheaded in the moonlight. I'll be glad to tell you where he is now. Wagner, Chopin . . . " He broke off his improvisation as fruitless, and after an audible swallow of brandy grunted apologetically and said, "Death is the commonest thing in the universe. What was this girl to you?"

"I was in love with her."

He writhed about in his chair, like a man being strapped into it for execution. "Oh, dear."

"I suppose you don't like to hear any more about these attachments than you have to, but they do develop. What are we supposed to do?"

"Where did you go, for heaven's sake?"

"In the garage. The pickup truck."

He sipped his brandy warily, as though on the lookout for emotional ambush everywhere. We faced one another in the wingbacks flanking the revived fire. I gathered that I had at least cleared myself of the charge of romanticism by admitting I was in love. It was realism he was up against. The old irony curled his lips as he said: "Did you kiss her?"

"Of course."

"You may live to regret it. Or then again, you may not," he added with one of his grim little jokes.

I set my brandy down and said: "Dr. Simpson, do you believe in a God?"

He just perceptibly raised his eyes, as if in entreaty to Heaven to spare him at least this. It took me some years to attain his mood and understand my blunder. He resented such questions as people do who have thought a great deal about them. The superficial and the slipshod have ready answers, but those looking this complex life straight in the eye acquire a wealth of perception so composed of delicately balanced contradictions that they dread, or resent, the call to couch any part of it in a bland generalization. The vanity (if not outrage) of trying to cage this dance of atoms in a single definition may give the weariness of age with the cry of youth for answers the appearance of boredom. Dr. Simpson looked bored as he ground his teeth and gazed away.

"Oh, one man's opinion about these things is as good as another's," he said. "You believe what you must in order to stave off the conviction that it's all a tale told by an idiot. You know, of course, you took a chance with that girl."

"It was worth it," I retorted, bitterly.

I finished my brandy and left the good doctor to his rest. A wind had come out of the north, and I hurried up the path through the cottage wood lot toward the dark hospital grounds, where winter clutched in his tight fist the flowers of May.

eight

THE WORLD, as has been noted, is full of a number of things, and while they may not suffice to keep us happy as kings, the troubles in which they mainly abound are diverse enough for one to distract us from the other. I had scarcely dried my tears for Rena when letters began to arrive from home indicating, at first in disquieting hints, then unmistakably, that my father was going out of his mind.

His first symptoms had been a worsening of his insomnia, and shortened patience with any breakfast-table assurances that he had dozed off once or twice during the night. Wakefulness was further vexed by a compulsive remembrance of things past; he would shake my mother to inquire the name of a landlord they had once had, or of a butcher whom they had long ago patronized. He would rout her from bed in the middle of the night to pore with him over road maps and atlases in search of some town they had visited years before, or merely stopped in for lunch. He literally racked his brains — as his headaches and head noises attested. Cajoleries and protests prompted by my mother's own fatigue and eventual hysteria were met with vehemence, then threats of violence. Once she found him in the kitchen at three o'clock in the morning swatting cockroaches with her brassière. To the aforementioned, add what was happening on the route. There he had taken to picking up garbage from one stop and leaving it at another. I had often longed to do some such thing myself, as a kind of passionate outcry, or gesture, against the Way Things Are, but as it was, my father's didoes, whether impromptu or deliberate, hardly amused the customers and were anything but good for business. Cancellations began to pour in as the peculiar "deliveries" continued. It was this development that brought a letter from Doc Berkenbosch.

That our family physician was himself trying to keep abreast of contemporary trends was amply reflected in this document, which suggested that guilt for his sins was what prompted the torments my father was inflicting on his fellow men. Scientific as the diagnosis sounded (and who could ask for a more consummate synthesis of Calvin and Freud?), I tended to doubt it. In any case Doc's letter was troubled, even urgent, and his frantic "Are you maybe not now well enough to come home and handle Pa?" sent me into action. I left the sanitarium without asking Dr. Simpson's permission, or even waiting for my next quarterly examination, due in a fortnight. I simply packed up and went.

Riding home on the Burlington Zephyr, I watched the scenery slip by and tried to remember happier days. The times my father took us all to the ice cream parlor; the characteristic cool, creamy smell of that place, so distinct from and yet so curiously similar to that in the saloons to which, in harsher hours, I was sent to fetch him home. Louie and I had often discussed these two smells, and decided that what they had in common was probably something picked up from the sawdust to be found on the floor in either haven. Sometimes it was nothing worse than a chili parlor in which I finally tracked Pa down, and then he would treat me to a bowl of it before coming along. Chili con carne was his favorite food, of which he often took a quart home to wash down with bottles of beer. My most vivid, if not tenderest, memory was of a night when he fell with his face in a plate of it.

It was about ten o'clock, and he was sitting at the kitchen table considerably the worse for several whiskeys which had, in this instance, preceded the beer and the chili standing ready for him, the one cold and other hot. He was in something of a daze, indeed on the verge of falling asleep over his dinner. It was nerve-racking to watch his eyes droop shut and his head nod each time an inch closer to the plate before snapping back. Feeling compassion for him, I looked away. If I removed the plate of chili he would land with his head on the hard table; if I shook him he would strike out blindly as he always did when roused in this condition and possibly do me bodily harm, which he would later regret. To counterbalance his drinking and his doubts he was doubly strict with himself about denying us the pleasures forbidden by the church, so that we were barred absolutely from the movies; but I had caught enough snatches of the cinema through open fire-escape and lobby doors to know that what we had here was the classic suspense of the short subject — a man swaying ever more perilously on a column of crates, or careening progressively farther over the edge of a cliff. With each foggy nod my father's face came closer to the plate, in which predestined goal it finally did land with a *splat* that sent beans and juice in all directions across the table top. The impact made his next galvanized awakening conclusive, and, revived, he sat up and ate like a trencherman, after using his bandanna at some length. But the incident satisfied fully the intellectuals' definition of the grotesque as a blend of the tragic and the comic.

I do not remember whether or not that was in one of his deeply pious intervals, hence whether grace was said over the hastily reassembled supper. Prayers at table were, among us, of a length usually encountered only in church among folk of more tepid faiths, for blessings invoked were by no means restricted to the food but included the church itself, its missions and the heathen they served, and a wide variety of secular matters. Thus in my father's devout periods, when he outdid the longest-winded clergymen, guidance was besought for the President and his Cabinet, legislatures both state and federal, as well as emissaries engaged on diplomatic undertakings then in the news, while the food itself grew cold in its bowls. I cannot remember eating anything but cold roast beef and cold chicken when my father was in one of his revivals. I once proposed that the dinner be kept in the oven until grace had been said, or if custom required that we encircle it formally while commending it to divine care, that we gather around the stove to say it, and was given a sound clap on the head for my impertinence.

The day after the chili con carne episode, I asked my father for half a dollar to go bowling, which remorse for his spree of the night before made him roundly deny me. We were one happy family dedicated to each other's welfare in mutual faith, and he was not going to compound a lapse into his cups by the sinful expenditure of money on frivolities and bodily exercise, which, as St. Paul had said, "counteth for little." My father was nothing if not thoroughgoing; superficiality was a charge that could never be brought against him. He heeded literally the injunction that one's religion ought to embrace all walks of life; he never brought us home anything flippant, and remembered his family but sparingly at Christmastime, and his friends not at all, on the ground that crass commercialism should not envelop the birth of our Lord. His habit of striking blows for the original meanings of things included Halloween, when we would at divine worship commemorate the origins of the Reformation, not squander money on masks and costumes. My father himself always stoutly denied that his conversion had any economic root, laying it rather to the direct intervention of a Providence who often spoke to us through narrow escapes. An example was to be found in an explosion in a garage at a time when my father normally, but not that day, passed through the alley there with his truck. "If I'd been fifteen minutes earlier I'd been blown to pieces, thank God," he said.

I thought of all these things in my train seat and while lying in my berth at night, and I was still thinking of them as I climbed the stairs with my luggage to the second-floor flat where we lived, the familiar smell in the hallway coiling about my vitals like a reptile.

Pa was waiting for me at the head of the stairs, ready to give me some idea of the nature and scope of his suffering. He wore incompatible slippers and, for a bath-robe, an old topcoat, under which was a black turtle-neck sweater. "You look awful," I said, to please him, and also to stem the tide of exposition, at least temporarily. It was after I had greeted him and kissed my mother, and we were settled once again in the old cold parlor, that he crossed his legs, gazed at the electric heater glowing on the floor nearby, and plunged into an account of some of the things that were troubling him.

"Ninety per cent of the universe is missing," he said, after a rehearsal of perturbations more familiar to me, which I paid no more heed than one does complaints one has heard for years like an old phonograph record played over and over. This was a new note, at which I pricked up my ears and glanced at my mother.

I learned later that day that what he had said was far from a figment of his imagination, but rather a scientific fact that appealed to it. I read, in the same morning paper he must have, a report of an astronomers' conven-tion at which a paper had been read making the point that the total gravitational force as calculated among the movements of celestial bodies needs, to account for it, nine or ten times more cosmic matter than we know about. Hence, ninety per cent of the universe is missing, at least from human computations, scattered through space or existing in dispersed forms beyond our ken. "We too may be dispersed, till we don't exist," my father said later, dilating on the matter. Knowing this fear to be shared by many reputable scientists, I felt a little easier. "Maybe that's hell — what they can't locate. Flung away from God, outer darkness. Black light! Antimatter! It's all around us. We're all headed for it!" Then he added, becoming more personal, "The only thing that keeps me from killing myself is the will to live."

This was from Doc Berkenbosch. Doc had, as noted, been grooming himself in at least the terminology of that profession into which his own now so often imperceptibly shaded. That was commendable. What was regrettable was that usually all he supplied was the terminology, and that flung about with no more precision than he had always accorded his own. He had a little modish information about the self-obliterative drive, which he explained existed in all of us in the form of a "blatant tendency," that is to say, a hidden or potential one, held in check in the majority of us. I also had "functional" explained to me. "Means mental, originating in the mind rather than the body. The meaning of the word is widening rapidly. You hear of modern architecture being functional. In other words, crazy."

The job of spreading confusion on two fronts kept Doc Berkenbosch twice as busy as he had been in the old days of simple medicine, and he left to my solution the problem of finding a sanitarium for my father which was both nearby and not too larcenous in cost for what would be, at the very least, a period of observation. Doc gave me the names of several, which I investigated in such time as remained from my second, scarcely less urgent problem, that of repairing the apostasies among the customers on the garbage route — which of course I now took over in full as the family's sole means of livelihood. I finally decided on one situated just beyond the city limits, five miles from home.

That the choice was a mistake was hardly my fault. One's search for such a place is always desperate and the investigation therefore superficial. They are all clean, all landscaped, all state-inspected. The inspections of the authorities in the case of Hilltop Haven, however, must have been as cursory as my own preliminary look. A few days after my father had been "admitted" (that fine institutional euphemism for arrivals which are usually forcible and sometimes police-assisted), I had a talk about him with the chief doctor. In the course of this chat, the gist of which was that the doctor would not be so irresponsible as to commit himself on the case on such short acquaintance, the doctor was called out of the office a moment, during which I had a chance to steal a glance at some charts on his desk. On one, after the word "Diagnosis," was the entry: "Nervous wreck." Still another of the reports I managed hastily to shuffle through contained the comment on a woman patient: "Seems crabbier than ever." Later in the corridor I saw two orderlies, or possibly two functionaries of higher rank, talking about a new arrival who I was certain was my father. One of them raised his hand and with a forefinger executed a significant circular motion at his temple.

I took my father straight out of that place (which by now I had learned was known among the neighborhood children as Chock Full o' Nuts) and drove him to the institution operated by our church. We had wished to avoid that because it was in Michigan, too far for the frequent, indeed daily, visits on which my mother was determined. But the move turned out immeasurably for the best. Not only was the establishment well run by a staff of competent psychiatrists (as church institutions usually are), but it developed that repeated visits by the family were not in the best interest of the patient, at least in the early stages of confinement. So it was with a sigh of relief, through our tears, that we turned out of the hospital driveway onto the main road, my mother and I, and headed for what was left of home.

There seems to be little support in reality for the popular belief that we are mellowed by suffering. Happiness mellows us, not troubles; pleasure, perhaps, even more than happiness. The sentimental saw belongs among those canards that include also the idea that wisdom comes with age. The old have nothing to tell us; it is more commonly we who are shouting at them, in any case.

These somewhat cynical observations may themselves be taken as possessing a selfish root, for they are prologue to the admission that suffering had certainly not mellowed me, and that I took precious little of my elders' advice about what to do with my life at this stage of it. I might better justify myself by pleading simply that I was still young at the time, of which it must be said that Rena was soon forgotten in my pursuit, resumed where it had been left off, of girls. I cannot honestly find it in my heart to say that her death or my father's disintegration "taught" me anything, or sobered me much. That remained for a more shattering bereavement still far off in time.

The trials under which I now labored were not unmixedly such, since they absolved me from the obligation to court with marriage in view. No girl could reasonably expect a man to add to the expenses under which I groaned those of a wife and family. My parents "came first." Too, I now had the advantage of a tainted heritage uppermost among those elements working for me as factors calculated to discourage husband hunters. Thus the intimacies I did contract — in which these drawbacks were "paid out" little by little as need required — I was free to enjoy, much as I had always liked to, without the onus of threatening entanglements. Any hopefuls not sifted out by these considerations were confronted with my ace in the hole: "I am a garbage man." Naturally this fact was held in reserve until absolutely necessary, when its disclosure was usually terminal: the scraping up of new acquaintance was contingent on its concealment, of course. Claim could also in a pinch be laid to a slight history of tuberculosis, though new X rays revealed the ailment to be completely arrested, if it had ever existed as anything more than a slight surplus of the bacillus known to exist in all of us at one time or another.

There was one environment in which this background was not stigmatic, but there no defense against the shibboleths of morality was needed since they were never invoked. This was the world of intellectuals who had become "Marxist-oriented" in a time which was now the Great Depression.

I did not return to the University, but I did now and again seek out the company of old friends in and around the campus, where, as I say, times had changed. A social conscience was requisite to even the most elementary pretense to a mental and artistic life. Writers and painters marched in parades demanding jobs, not, to be sure, for themselves, but at least for others; students attended political rallies and sometimes addressed them. There lived, in an obscure South Side street not far from the Midway, a group of artists who maintained close touch with those on the North Side, where the backbone of Chicago Bohemianism lay, whose roots went back to the days of Ben Hecht and Maxwell Bodenheim and the old Dill Pickle Club. The club was gone now, but Bughouse Square, where the soapbox rebels foregathered, lived on, and it was thither we repaired every Saturday night to express and further the new iconoclasm.

In this milieu, of course, my immigrant and proletarian origins were a badge of honor, while my working on a garbage truck made me a downright hero. And well it might, for I was the only one in the bunch who had ever done an honest day's work in his life. Everyone in it was a fellow traveler of the Communist party, and some were members of it. I was once asked soon after my admission to the group whether I "carried a card." The term was new to me, and in my innocence I thought it was being used in the traditional salesman's sense, that is, of commercial cards carried on the person for purposes of identification and to drum up trade. "No," I said, "but I may have to get some printed if business gets any worse." I was serious, but the laughter which greeted my reply established me instantly as a wag of great promise.

Benefits were often held for worthy causes, such as the New Masses or some ex-convict folk singer or indigent poet, usually in the form of a party at which admission was charged and some hope of entertainment held out, generally a performance or reading by the artist himself. On more occasions than might have been thought possible this was Maxwell Bodenheim, though on neither of the two on which I went to hear him read from his verses did he show up, at least in the living room. "He's still out," a girl announced to us once after returning from a bedroom into which she had slipped to check on the guest of honor. I dropped my dollar into the hat anyway with a smile; I was seeing life.

Life unfolded, for so footloose a youth in a time so out of joint, as a series of romances as inconclusive as I could have hoped and as unsatisfying as might be guessed. There was Lucia, who passed the hat — a girl always remorselessly dressed in black, and with black hair and eyes herself, a resulting monochrome which perhaps devisedly emphasized her beautiful clear white skin. There was Peggy Shotzinoff, a dancer in a local ballet troupe. Not the classic ballet, but that species of calisthenics executed in tight jeans and bare feet and addressing itself to contemporary problems such as soil erosion or the installation of high-tension wires through valleys in which people have hitherto lived in peace. There was . . . But why go on with the recital of what were no more and no less, no better and no worse, than the next youth's wild oats: a series of entr'actes in search of a drama. I mention them at all merely to suggest that I went through the normal pursuits of profane love before entering upon the sacred.

I use the term loosely, as should be, since any sanctity into which my foolish years at last emerged, or to which I — or any man — may validly lay claim, is not fleshly, but paternal. But that is getting ahead of the story. The marriage comes next. I met the girl who was to become my wife in the most unexpected place.

nine

I WAS VISITING my father one Sunday afternoon in late spring when, the intermittently shining sun having appeared to come out to stay, he rose from the window chair in which he had been dejectedly slumped and said, "Let's go for a walk." I bundled him into a coat, and we were released into the open air by an orderly with a set of keys.

I was pleased to find this turn of mood in my father, who had for months been so steeped in depression that no show of interest in anything could be excited in him, least of all a walk. The sanitarium grounds were pleasant, cool in the shadows but warm enough in the sun to which we kept, and as we coursed among the glimmering shrubbery he began to brighten further, even to the extent of greeting a few of his cronies, likewise promenading in the company of dear ones.

The novelty of the walk having worn off, my father resumed those protestations and complaints which were often all that ever broke his silences. They came on in familiar waves, to which one need not lend more than half an ear. His head ached, there was this "sour feeling" in his legs, his back killed him. He had a chest cold for which nothing did any good; cough medicine made him cough. Racking his memory for names was more than he could bear. My own back was killing me, truth to tell, after two nights in a motel with beds that were nothing to brag about. "I've got spots in front of my eyes," he said.

"I can see them," I answered, which was not as heart-less as it may sound.

As we traversed what remained of a lane leading to-ward the women's building, looking for a vacant bench in the sun, I saw, a short distance ahead, a couple whom I recognized. They were Mr. and Mrs. Wigbaldy. I had not seen them since my return from the West, since I neither attended church nor frequented any other circles where our paths might cross. The meeting was rather awkward. As they inquired about my father — receiving no dearth of answers for their pains — I appraised them, wondering who was visiting whom. While both had aged a little, neither visibly bore the scars of disturbance or hospitalization. As we talked, my father spotted an in-mate who had recently left his ward and whom he was eager to see, and he darted over to greet him. I took the moment to ask:

"What brings you two here?"

They turned simultaneously and indicated a solitary figure seated on a bench behind them. It was a moment before I recognized Greta, or acknowledged that I did. She had lost considerable weight, and her face wore the expression of utter listlessness that one often encounters in such an environment, not to be confused with more aggressive depression such as my father's. She had on a kind of housedress, over which was an unbuttoned coat. One hand lay, palm up, in her lap. She squinted into the sun as we made our way over to her.

"Hello, Greta."

"Hello, Don." She answered indifferently, not extending her hand or otherwise moving on the bench. I myself therefore sat down on it beside her, as did her mother. Wigbaldy remained standing a few steps off.

"How long have you been here?"

"About a month," Mrs. Wigbaldy answered tersely for her. She seemed to have collected herself in an assertive readiness to answer any questions I might have, which I found disquieting.

"In for a little rest, are you?"

Greta nodded. "So they say." She smiled faintly. "How are you?"

"I'm all right. O.K." There was a pause, during which I gazed rather inanely down at two or three pigeons strutting about on the gravel path. "How long will you be here? Do they give you any idea?"

Here her vague manner changed abruptly. She spoke in a rapid whisper, looking around her as she did. "It depends. If they'd only stop it — the men. I'd run away, but where would I go? It would always be the same, the men looking at you everywhere. Their eyes, you can feel them, crawling over you like bugs."

She looked off in the direction of the women's building, in the doorway of which a nurse in a white uniform was beckoning her over for something. The Wigbaldys and I watched her go, till the glass door had closed behind her and the nurse both. Mrs. Wigbaldy now turned back to me. We were both on our feet again.

"Well, now you can see what you've done. I hope you're satisfied."

Wigbaldy said something indistinct, little more than an apologetic clearing of his throat, as he shuffled a few more feet away on the path. He was openly miserable.

"I had no idea . . . " I shook my head in pained confusion. "You mean that . . . "

Mrs. Wigbaldy nodded, her mouth a tight seam.

"She never got over the experience. It dirtied her. It dirtied her foul." Mrs. Wigbaldy faced me squarely now, wringing every drop from every word. "It dirtied her good, what you started her out on."

"Why didn't she write me?"

"She did a few times, but all the good it did her."

"I didn't answer regular letters, no — it wouldn't have been fair to her. But nobody told me about this."

"It only just come up," Wigbaldy threw in over his shoulder.

"And she had more pride. Anyhow, now you know what can happen to a girl when she gets mixed up with a — tramp!" Mrs. Wigbaldy turned on her heel and marched into the building.

Wigbaldy shook his head, as though deploring crime and punishment alike. He seemed to be prodding something in the grass with the toe of his shoe. "Don't judge yourself too hard, boy. We all know it takes two." In his awkwardness he seemed to me a symbol of eternally cheated mankind, of all betrayed decency. This estimate was slightly more than the facts warranted, since it turned out I was being railroaded and he knew it. All the same, he may have felt, without too much casuistry in his heart, that I had that coming to me. We often deserve our injustices; after all, we get away with murder.

Feeling that facts rather than hysterical charges were what I needed, I went in to see the psychiatrist in charge of Greta as soon as I had returned my father to his ward. This doctor shrugged a great deal, not as a man declaring ignorance of the answers or shirking the questions, but as if pleading the eternally constant, eternally elusive human element that makes everything unique and unpredictable. He accompanied each shrug with a gesture of spreading his hands above his shoulders, as though with each question I were "holding him up" for answers he had not truly in his possession.

"She's been in a sort of funk as a result of a mess with a man. She felt, oh, not defiled by the experience. Well, yes, defiled. We're often too quick to use the medical word 'ego.' Why not say her pride was shattered? Her woman's self-respect."

"Can it be restored?"

Now he really did "put 'em up" and, in keeping with the rules of his profession, declined advising directly. "All I will say is that I don't think it's too deep-seated, or necessarily permanent. Just a bad emotional tailspin that given the right circumstances she could pull out of. Or that someone could help pull her out of. Obviously a good relationship would be better than any medicine of ours." The nature of my questions emboldened him to ask one of his own. "Were you involved with her?"

"Could it be family standards that came down on her like a ton of bricks, rather than the so-called sin itself?" I asked, declining to answer.

"Just what do you mean?"

"Could Mama be at the bottom of the trouble? *Coaching* her into shame?"

This was so completely a stick-up that he flung his arms wide with a laugh. "That's a large order, especially since Greta's only been here a few weeks and I haven't even met the mother."

"Don't break your neck."

I may very well have spared the doctor the pleasure. I saw Greta on each of the four successive weekends I ran up there to visit my father. I received, I sensed, some unobtrusive co-operation from Wigbaldy, who saw to it that our talks on the green grass were not hampered by the presence of Mama. Each time Greta seemed a little better, a little rosier of cheek, brighter in spirit. She became her old self — a description not to be left unqualified by the reminder that she had always had a pensive and even somber side. Indeed, it had been her kind of brooding voluptuousness that had first attracted me to her. At last I asked her to marry me.

She pulled a dandelion from the lawn on which we were sitting and flung it away. "Don't feel you have to."

"No such thing. I ought to settle down too. And we did have some pretty good times together."

"We strike fire where that's concerned. Well, all right, let's. Sure, Don."

She blossomed under the agreement, as, truth to tell, did I, after what seemed now a feckless and fruitless period of my life. My relief at the decision was more than the moral elation of one from whose skies the clouds of guilt have blown. Greta, her buxom bloom recovered, left the sanitarium one Sunday afternoon and drove back to Chicago with me.

My mother died just around that time, and feelings of sympathy toward me drew Greta farther out of her shell. Attending the funeral, in fact, was her first re-emergence in our community. All the emotions in which we had so far been clogged and choked suddenly broke free, like a fire that stops smoking and catches ablaze. We set a date, showers were sprung on her by fluttering girl friends, and invitations issued.

It was in the midst of this whirl of preparation that I received a mysterious and anonymous note in the mail. It was written in ink on a scrap of paper evidently torn from a sheet of foolscap, and read: "Do you know about her past?"

After my first burst of anger had cooled somewhat, I experienced a moment of wry amusement. Who but I, after all, had contributed to that past? Thus my informant, whoever he was, had unwittingly addressed his warning to the culprit rather than the victim. But then his (or her) not knowing the actual truth began itself to eat at me, as did my not knowing the identity of the writer. This uncertainty harrowed me for days. What troubled me too was a nagging familiarity about the handwriting. Whose was it? Where had I seen it before? I longed to show the note to Greta, but of course chivalry barred that resort. Then one evening the mystery was added to. After a week of stewing, during which Greta had struck me as behaving rather nervously herself, she asked me point-blank whether I had received an anonymous communication in the mail. Feeling that this released me from knightly obligations, I showed her the note.

"I wrote it," she said.

"What kind of game is this?"

"It's not a game. There's something I've got to tell you."

"Please do."

She poured us stiff highballs, a unique measure in those parts and feasible only because her parents were out and unable to protest such use of the family medicinal bottle. We both paced the room, our glasses tinkling merrily throughout the following far from festive passage.

"After you went away, I had an affair with a man," Greta related. "Nobody you know. He wasn't Dutch Reformed. It was the boss in the office where I had a job for a short while. I got pregnant and had to go away and — " Here her voice broke as she lowered her head in tears. I waited for her to pull herself together and continue.

"Where I went — I can't say 'we' because he behaved like a perfect cad — I won't say. Some place out of the state. I left the child in the home there and — that's all there's to it, really. He was married. Not that he couldn't have helped out with a little money. Men can be rats, all right, just as women can be fools. I don't know which is worse."

"Does anybody know about this?" I asked in a voice that seemed to be strained through some kind of dense but immaterial batting temporarily stopping my mouth.

"In Chicago? Not a soul."

"How about the writer of the note?"

"You still don't believe I wrote it. Just a sec."

She went to her bedroom, where through the chattering of my ice cubes I heard a drawer being slid open. She returned holding in her hand the remainder of the sheet of paper from which the note had been torn. She set the two fragments side by side on a table and matched them into a whole, like parts of a treasure map of which individual pirates hold only a portion, requiring validation by the group as a unit.

"Why didn't you tell me without going through all this rigmarole?"

"I couldn't. I tried over and over to get up the courage, but the words just wouldn't out. You know that feeling. I had to have them dragged out of me. I wished some busybody would tell you about it, so they would be. Like if you'd get an anonymous note or something. So I wrote such a note, and now the thing has been dragged out of me. It may sound crazy to you, but it's off my conscience."

"Conscience! You seem to have one that's easily satisfied."

"Please don't. You're free to go now. I won't hold you to anything."

"After the invitations are out! A fine thing that would be, wouldn't it? What a rat that would make me out. You waited till I was nicely hemmed in by — "

"Oh, please!" Her voice broke again. "Can't you imagine what I've been through? If they seem tricks I played, let them prove how desperate I've been to keep you. I begin to see only now how much I've wanted you. The engagement needn't bother you. I'll say I broke it. That's what's done in these cases. If you think you'd be getting damaged goods — "

"Oh, that's not the point, and you know it. We don't hold one another to virginity any more — and wouldn't I be a great one to. The fact that you got into a mess doesn't make any difference."

"You mean you don't mind?"

"Oh, Greta, of course I mind. In the same way you do. The affair itself was just an affair. It could happen to — "

Here my train of thought broke off, interrupted by a burst of illumination about another aspect of all this. The revelation must have shone in my face, for Greta looked at me and said, "What's the matter?"

"Then it wasn't I who caused your nervous breakdown. It was him."

"Yes."

"Pretty lousy of your parents to make me think I was the villain."

"That's why I had to tell you."

"It doesn't absolve them. What's their excuse for doing me this dirt?"

"Old-fashioned morality."

"Come again, please?"

"They figure you were ultimately responsible. You set me on the primrose path."

"A likely name for it!" I dropped into a chair, feeling as though I were being physically stoned. "Does their position make any sense? I mean I'd rather it did. I mean one would rather think he was a stinker than be getting them for in-laws. So explain it to me a little more. Justify it."

"It's perfectly simple if you look at it in their light. You were my first. You seduced me, or whatever word you want to use. All the rest followed from that. Therefore, the child that resulted from an affair I might not have had if it hadn't been for you might as well be yours. It *is* yours morally," she concluded, taking on rather the tone her mother herself might have in this summation, were she capable of decent English.

"Can you get it back?"

"No. It's too late for that. Oh, Don, don't let's torture ourselves with that. I for one have certainly been through enough." She bent her head again, moaning the last words, and twisting her fingers about in her lap. She had set her drink down and was seated beside me on the sofa. "You're sure you . . . "

"After all we've been through? The world is too many for me, baby. God knows I can't make head or tail of it alone. I doubt whether two people can either, but I guess there's no harm in their trying."

We sat a moment in the deepening dusk. There were no lamps lit. As I brooded on all that had happened, and was happening, still another aspect of the whole situation struck me as deserving an airing now while everything was terrible anyway. Greta was quite herself again on the surface, but who could guess what might not lie beneath, what rocks and tangled growth composed the bottom of this calm sea. I therefore thought the point worth bringing up.

"Do you think people should marry if there is any — well, nervous history?" I asked.

She slipped an arm around me and drew my head toward her.

"Silly boy," she said. "It's not your father I'm marrying. It's you."

I sold the disposal route for five thousand dollars to a church elder who owned a chain of them, and with the money finished my college education, of which only a year remained. I did not return to the University of Chicago but enrolled in a downtown school with a lower tuition and a good business-administration department. Wigbaldy had advised me in the sale and offered to help me in any tiding over I might later need in my transition to a better career — which was decent of him, though hardly more than the family owed me in the circumstances.

There was a slight skirmish over religious matters, which I thought it best to have out in a preliminary way at least. For one thing, I proposed a civil ceremony. I was clamorously reminded that you can't have such a thing at a wedding. I yielded this point, sensing that Greta was only trying to spare her parents' feelings, not hewing to views of her own which might clash with mine. But I made an issue of the precise wording of the vows. I wanted liberalized ones, with no outmoded Pauline nonsense exacting from the bride the promise to "obey" the groom. Here I put my foot down, rather in the manner of a husband determined to show at the outset who was boss. "I'll have no obedience around here!" I said, banging the table. "Is that clear?"

"Is it an order?"

"Yes."

"But you can't ask Reverend Van Scoyen to use any but the official church form."

"I suppose you're right."

The danger of our being given a model home was narrowly averted, Wigbaldy having just sold the last "unit" in his latest development, preliminary to doing a little traveling with the profits. In fact, he and Mrs. Wigbaldy were sailing for Holland two days after the wedding — "a second honeymoon for the missus and me." Our honeymoon consisted of a week end at the Windermere, that Hyde Park hostelry whose name, you may recall, had always so potently conjured the Worldly life I had from boyhood promised myself, and which in young manhood I had sighted more closely as, dallying on the rocks at Lake Michigan, I had gazed northward at the lights along the shore.

We made the most of our few days there, dining the first evening on roast pheasant and champagne at a table laid in a window of our room affording a long, sweeping view to the south. Greta insisted on having a second bottle sent up after we had polished off the first, and nursing that, we talked about where we might like to look for an apartment. We were to stay in the Wigbaldys' bungalow for the three months of their absence, during which period we would have to conduct our hunt. Rentals were scarce.

Carrying her glass, Greta came around and knelt beside my chair. She nibbled the lobe of my ear. "We'll live at the foot of Gingerbread Lane, in a house nailed together with cloves."

This gave me rather a turn. My legs stiffened as with an old disquiet, a kind of horror almost, under the table. Then I laughed as I realized to my relief that she was drinking far more than was good for her.

ten

MIDWAY THROUGH the second year of our marriage my wife had a religious conversion. She left the church and joined another.

The impression that this is nothing at all could arise only from the ignorance of one unversed in the rigors of orthodox indoctrination. The thing indicated *fervor* — more fervor than is required lackadaisically to stay on. It indicated a freshet of emotion strong enough to drive her out of a denomination whose dogmas she could not honestly embrace into one whose tenets she could. I should not speak of tenets in the plural. "No creed but Christ" was the slogan of the temple, revivalistic in nature, which twice each Sunday and once in midweek she helped throng. Thus was ended a conformity based on "custom and superstition," as the Dutch dominees themselves called an adherence to outward forms, in favor of a church against which, however, their strictures were even more vehement: one which did not preach, for instance, the elementary Christian principle of infant damnation.

Greta's move seemed the emotional product of our failure to have any children, either to damn or to save. She thought her barrenness a punishment for having had one which she had not kept — though keeping it would have required her confessing, before a slavering congregation, the sin of adultery. The change was made in the face of all my pleas to "give me time" — a chivalrous recognition that sterility is as often as not the man's. No dice. I did not protest strongly beyond a certain point, seeing no objection to married couples going their separate ways on the subject of religion provided there are no children over whose rearing the split can become fatal. Ours did not, as I say, meet that requirement.

The difference between us arose, not over the conversion as such, but over the misconduct with the bygone employer the memory of which had motivated it. She now spoke of it obsessively as a sin. I continued to view it as a simple indiscretion, and with a broad-minded tolerance for which I was sharply rebuked and which, as her piety waxed in intensity, she called on me to repent. This I refused to do.

"I don't see how you can defend what I did," she said. "Sometimes I wonder whether you have any standards at all."

Our views on this score were irreconcilable. The Tabernacle evangelist to whom she had confessed her guilt, Reverend Tonkle, came to call on me to try to make me see the error of my ways. My attitude remaining, on this point, adamant, he expressed the wish to pray for me, whereupon we sank all three to our knees, I with them in the general emotion, since I saw no objection to extending a guest this courtesy. Ardent pleas for my soul were raised, and the hope expressed that my hardened heart would be softened by the sun of God's grace, to the end that the two joined by him in holy wedlock might live together in Christian fellowship. None of this altered the situation in the least. I went about my way "conniving at the deed" in question, unregenerate still.

"I forgive her," I said stubbornly.

"That is not the question. It's whether God will forgive you," Reverend Tonkle said. "It's your immoral attitude that's wrong."

"He was a *married man*, Don," Greta remonstrated.

"That was no worse than your being unmarried. Maybe his home life wasn't all it might have been. Maybe he was unhappy. I think these affairs impose a morality of their own."

"Oh!" she gasped in dismay. "May God forgive you for that."

"Be that as it may, I still think what I always have. *I do not condemn you.*"

This was too much for her, and for Reverend Tonkle too, and they both gave off for now with the assurance that they would continue to pray for me in future.

The gulf between Greta and me over these incompatible outlooks widened with my refusal to go to the Tabernacle — after, that is, the one or two services to which I accompanied her to jolly her along and to satisfy my curiosity. These left nothing to be desired in the way of Bible-banging evangelism. Any pentecostal tongues of fire she hoped to see descend upon me were dampened by the spectacle of Reverend Tonkle's tub thumping. They got results, as the number of those shuffling for-

139

ward to make "decisions for Christ" attested, but I was not among them.

Nothing can drive so deep a wedge between two people as the hostility of one toward beliefs held dear by the other, and matters went from bad to worse for Greta and me. Then, as suddenly as they had started, they began to clear up. Greta found herself unexpectedly pregnant, and I myself again unexpectedly cherished. Even my "moral attitude" was no longer deplored. In her radiance she became less disapproving of my refusal to go to church, then finally lax in attendance herself. This was all to the good. She now had something to keep her home.

Since we know so little about the roots of externals themselves mysterious, it may very well have been that her success in conceiving a child resulted in part from emotional fires set by her religion. I did not look a gift horse in the mouth, at any rate. The religion itself had played its role for one who, in addition, now had evidence that the hand of God had not stricken her with infertility as punishment for past transgressions. The winds of human instability blow us into unexpected havens. We picnicked in bed on Sunday nights now, with snacks of cheese and crackers and sardines and what not, washed down with mugs of cocoa, which I happily brewed. I was utterly at peace. One night as we lay glutted, watching her ripening stomach for signs of the infant kicking, as she liked to have me do, I remembered Louie and my uncle arguing over my pregnant aunt. The whole wrangle and its hysterical aftermath, when we thought my aunt was going to have the baby then and there, came back so vividly that I laughed. "What's so funny?" Greta asked. I told her the story.

She was instantly roused.

"You mean," she said, sliding up in bed and wadding the pillow behind her so that she might sit more comfortably, "the stages of evolution are enacted in a human *embryo?* That right now this baby is a reptile or something?"

I hedged, fearing that I had blundered onto a subject that was touchy in the light of her recent experience and might prove explosive. When I tried to choke it off, she persisted. "No, explain it to me. I'd like to hear more about it."

My account proved to be halting and inexpert. Seeing that sound scientific documentation was all that could get me through, I got out an old biology textbook and simply let her read the passages in question herself. She read for an hour or more, and with very little sign of being nonplused by the revelation. "Hmm," she said finally, laying the book face-down on her stomach. "The whole thing is kind of a miracle in itself. Very beautiful."

"Of course, Creation is Creation, whether it takes a week or a billion years."

So far from having her faith "shaken," therefore, she seemed to have been set aglow by the sense of wonders incarnate in her, a development which put me contrarily in the mood to thank Heaven. My relief was premature. The discovery brought Reverend Tonkle once again to our door, clutching in a pale hand his limp-leather Bible.

"Mrs. Wanderhope has been troubled, she tells me, by certain doubts," he began, losing no time after hanging his hat in the hall. Shades of my childhood! "Doubts

arising from things you've been telling her. It is necessary that offenses come, but woe to him by whom the
offenses come. It's a serious matter to shake a person's
faith."

"Her faith hasn't been shaken — just changed," I said.
"Wouldn't you put it that way, dear?" I asked Greta,
who was lying under a quilt on the living-room couch.
She nodded. She seemed untroubled and in the best of
spirits as she nibbled from a box of glazed fruit. She had
aired developments with Reverend Tonkle because she
felt she owed it to him after inquiries about her absence
from divine worship. Still, I had a suspicion that she
rather anticipated the pitched battle between the two
men. She certainly listened to it with rapt interest. There
is no need to reproduce it here, even in summary, since
it was an almost literal echo of the one between Louie
and my uncle with which these events begin. I leaned
heavily on Louie for arguments. In fact, I had at one
point the exhilarating feeling of Louie's living once again
in me as I flung out what I knew was an almost word-for-
word recollection of Louie's climax to my uncle, for it
was one of those childhood incidents branded deep into
one's memory:

"If you want to believe in a God who creates us to be
a land biped and then deliberately stuffs us with relics
of a marine past and a four-footed past we never had, in
order to confuse us or whatever, why go ahead. You're
welcome to Him!"

"I shall pray for you," Reverend Tonkle said.

"All right, but not here."

"Please, Don. Please, both of you."

"You see what you've done? Now we'll have no more

of this excitement. I don't want her to have any trouble."

By this time I had my college degree and was working in the Chicago branch of an Eastern advertising agency. By the time our daughter Carol was born we had been transferred to the main office in New York. Before we knew it Carol was a toddling three-year-old, and, my affairs having prospered within the modest range possible in that firm, we made the customary move into Westchester.

Greta's emotional sailing was far from smooth. Her attitude toward the child alternated between smothering bursts of affection and lapses into a kind of weary oblivion, when she would seem not to be aware that the girl was about, or that I was either. Her moods then ominously recalled that abstraction in which I had found her sitting on the bench on the hospital grounds that Sunday afternoon I had gone to visit my father.

One day, after reading an article by an amateur anthropologist, Greta complained that the suburbs were stifling her. So we gave a party to which more people were invited than there was room for in the house, and in the course of which we picked up invitations for three more such functions on successive Saturday nights. On the third, Greta, whose liquor consumption had been rising steadily, drank so much I had to carry her into the house and put her to bed. The broad Congregational face of Mrs. Brodhag, the maid, who was hanging over the banister in a woolen bathrobe, did little to brighten the occasion. The classic miseries of the morning after were varied with accusations to the effect that I was the real culprit.

"How do you figure that?"

"You saw me drinking too much but did nothing to stop it. In fact, there you were gaily *fetching* me the stuff. You must have known I was going to make a fool of myself. Oh, some of the things I said!"

"Nonsense. A good toot now and then does none of us any harm." I spoke with that tremulous nonchalance of one who knows he is in trouble, deep in a psychological problem for which all the transparent ruses of "using psychology" are worthless. "Ventilates us, gets things out of our system. You've been so blue lately I figured it'd do you good. But now you must be quiet."

"So now you approve of drunkenness," she mumbled. "You draw the line at nothing, do you?"

It appeared to be in the throes of hang-over that she got things out of her system, at least in this case. She was lying on her stomach and spoke out of one side of her mouth, the other being mashed into the pillow. She now twisted around onto her back, groaning with fresh accesses of dizziness entailed by this change of position.

"Your own wife making a spectacle of herself. I'd be ashamed."

"But darling, you looked nice there, dancing on the table with your skirts up."

"You have no shame whatever."

I went to the bathroom, where I dug an ice bag from the back of a shelf in the linen closet. I filled it with ice cubes in the kitchen, and when I returned I started to put it gingerly on her forehead. She took it from my hands abruptly, like Napoleon snatching the crown from Pope Pius at his coronation and setting it on his own head.

"Aren't you the least bit sorry?" she murmured, that done.

"Well, all right. I'll never let it happen again."

"Promise?"

"Promise."

"Because sometimes I wonder if I haven't married beneath me," she went on, in a manner causing me to question whether, in fact, she had yet reached the hangover stage. She gave her cap a last adjustment.

"You have. But now I know your capacity, and I'll watch it after this. Get some rest now. I've got to drive Carol to Louisa's house. They have a new burro."

One summer when Carol was attending day camp, Greta had an affair with a man named Mel Carter. He was an Eastern publicity representative for a film studio, and often instructed dinner parties to which we went in those days with accounts of the movies' coming of age. "We have a picture coming up," he said once, "in which a character says 'son of a bitch.' Lots of other exciting things are happening. Still, it's only a beginning. Much remains to be done." His morals were the equal of his intelligence, and, his antennae having sensed in Greta a Discontented Woman, he made frank overtures to her at a luncheon in the city to which he had secretly asked her. She was then going into New York quite frequently, ostensibly to look for some part-time modeling work. The facts did not come to my attention till that fall, but when they did, I said that Mrs. Wanderhope was my wife, a claim I was prepared to substantiate with gunfire. I was accused of narrow-minded intolerance and outmoded standards. Greta implemented these charges by thrusting at me a book by Bertrand Russell setting forth the civilized view that marriage ought perhaps to be regarded as permanent if at all possible, but not as excluding other relations. This drove me to the extreme of pitching into the hearthfire a work by one of our more provocative contemporary thinkers. Her conduct, and especially the shrill manner in which she defended it, should have reminded me that I was dealing with instability rather than infidelity, and caused me to behave more responsibly myself. Perhaps my nerves were frayed more than my pride was wounded. In any case, my behavior had the effect of frightening Mel Carter away for good. That in turn speeded Greta's erratic decline. At the height of one bitter altercation, she ran out of the house into the street, shouting imprecations. I went after her, feeling as though I had been sucked into a nightmare.

"Everything is awful!" she exclaimed when I had overtaken her. I grasped her by the arm and drew her to a halt. "What's the use? Why go on? What's the good of it, what's the point?"

"Easy, now. We all ask that at times, it's part of the human condition, but we all carry on."

"What for?"

We stood on the sidewalk, under the shedding maple trees.

"Think of Carol," I said.

"She'd be better off without me, and you know it."

"That kind of talk is begging the question. No child would be better off without a mother who thinks of it."

"That's what's so awful," she went on, ignoring this. "Girls' fathers mean more to them than their mothers."

This seemed to me so much one of those unsportsmanlike gambits for advantage by the self-pitying, the emotionally truant, that I said sharply, "Rubbish! I'll not listen to any more talk like that." She seemed to deflate, as she often did at the peaks of these discharges, and allowed herself to be led back to the house, like a runaway animal.

As we strolled grotesquely beneath the trees, I spoke to her quietly so as not to be overheard by neighbors or passers-by, though still grasping her firmly by the arm. "We have lots of good things ahead of us, lots to live for. And so you must pull yourself together, and go to someone who might help you, as soon as we can find one. Then shalt thou have thy summer's lease, nor Death brag thou wander'st in his shade," I said, turning to her with a smile.

"What?"

"Sonnet eighteen. Remember how we used to read them together, when you were pregnant and all? Let's build a good fire tonight and read them over again."

Shakespeare! Surely one deserved better than that.

The idea did not seem at first a very good one after we had begun to act on it. I read aloud for half an hour or more, during which she sat motionless in a chair and cried, the tears running uninterruptedly down her cheeks. When I stopped and laid the book aside, she nodded and smiled at me, and in one of those subtle shifts of mood that emphasize how much we live by one another's variable weather, I sensed that she might be wooed.

I took her by the hand and drew her upstairs where we crept past Mrs. Brodhag's closed door, looked into Carol's room long enough to draw up the covers kicked back in her sleep and to restore to her pillow a favorite animal fallen from her embrace to the floor, and thence into the harbor of our own bedroom. There were some prolonged and pleasant shenanigans, in the course of which Greta paused to appraise herself critically and ask whether she wasn't getting too heavy. Didn't I think the bit of modeling with which she had hoped to help pay for Mrs. Brodhag was now out of the question? I answered that thank God it was; that anyone who wanted the two-dimensional spooks to be seen in Vogue and Harper's Bazaar was welcome to them, but I preferred the Rubensian ideal, at least in a wife. "Oh, you Dutchmen," she said. "For a woman to satisfy you at home she has to be a disgrace in public." Then she wet her finger and touched her hip, the way women test the heat of a flatiron.

She refused to see a psychiatrist, seeing no need of one in her ups and resisting the idea during her downs, so that I wondered how her parents had managed this problem in bygone times. Then perhaps the matter had been less critical, and she herself more pliable. She became now steadily more unpredictable, sometimes disappearing for hours on a tour of the local and outlying pubs, once remaining away overnight, to be located, finally, in a highway motel in a room bearing evidence of other occupancy than her own.

What, one may ask, is the effect of such things on a child?

Our inability ever to guess with any confidence when children are hurt, and when not, by such emotional tests as we subject them to leaves them in somewhat the category of the human eyeball, that wonder about which doctors are said to be still theoretically undecided whether it is the tenderest or the toughest of human substances. I had no idea what impression we succeeded in making on our little girl, who was five at the time these troubles came to a head and six when her mother made good her threat forcibly to resign from human affairs. Late one night, when Greta had been fetched home from her bars and was permitting herself to be soothed and stilled in a kitchen embrace, I heard a stir behind the door to the dining room, which was swung back to the wall. Through the crack between the hinges I saw Carol smiling guiltily out at us while she lipsticked her mouth with a piece of scarlet crayon. "Aren't you in bed?" The tableau restored everyone's sanity for the time being, and we laughed, the three of us, as we drank hot chocolate at the kitchen table.

Carol had a charming habit of saying "Hi" every time she saw you in the house, even if she had so greeted you in another room five minutes before. You could not run into her often enough. What else? She said "You're welcome" to the grocer when, having counted out your change after a purchase, he said "Thank you." She universalized other courtesies in which she had been instructed, such as not pointing in public. She once accused me of not practicing what I preached when I indicated some artistically disposed gourds and maple leaves in the autumn window of Mr. Hawley's dry goods store; I thought better of explaining that the amenity was not intended to include natural or inanimate objects, but only people. It is amazing how much parental love is embodied in laughter at the object. Carol's mother and I had to leave the room on the occasion of her fourth-birthday party when we saw her lean toward a celebrant in a dress with a colossal bow behind and say, "If you're going to be sick, may I have your orange slices?" Within a few years Carol was able to laugh in this way herself about other children. She told me this story about a neighbor boy named Merton Mills. Merton had promised his parents a telephone stand for Christmas which he would make with his own two hands in manual training. After some weeks he was asked how it was coming along, and he said fine, though slowly. As the holidays neared, he said in response to further inquiries that he had run into some snags but would have the handiwork in time; in addition to the construction, of course, there would be finishing touches, such as a coat of lacquer and some decalcomania trim. Things like that. When Christmas itself rolled around and there was still no telephone stand, he explained that they would have to be disappointed. "Someone stole the materials," he said.

What, I thought to myself as I gazed at Carol, if anything should happen to that creature? Looking back, we seem to detect clairvoyance in certain moments of apprehension, but mine were no more than pass like a chill over the heart of any parent watching his treasure asleep in bed or taking off down the road on a bicycle, which we call premonitions by hindsight if our fears materialize. A neighbor had been robbed by the Fates of a nine-year-old boy whom I will unabashedly describe as hyacinthine-haired, and a year later was still inconsolable to the point of unfitness for human society. I reminded him sharply that he had three other children, and he turned on me with clenched fists. "There aren't enough children in the world to make a dent in grief for one," he said. I had little suspicion then that I would be crying foul myself, under terms more final than his own. This being then foreshadowed, I can say, like the narrator in *Our Town*, "I reckon you know what the third act is about."

We had for a few months then an old dog, left us by a family who had moved to Florida, on which Carol doted, and which she stoutly defended as "part pedigree." By moving a table morsel from side to side in mid-air, she could make the mesmerized beast shake his head in the negative as she asked it, "Do you like Mommy? Do you like Daddy?" and by swinging the tidbit up and down as she asked, "Do you like me?" cause it to nod yes. She turned six that winter, becoming more than ever Tuesday's Child, so full of grace, so poised that, as a friend of ours remarked, you could hold her on your outstretched palm and she would balance perfectly. There is a point when life, having showered us with jewels for nothing, begins to exact our life's blood for paste. That was the point I had now reached.

One Saturday in June, after Greta had been drinking heavily for two days, I found her slumped over the wheel of the car in the closed garage with the motor running. I rushed to open the door, which stuck as my fingers clawed at the handle and my head burst with a lungful of held breath. I got it open at last and raced to the nearby hospital, fortunately in time. Why say "fortunately"? After six months in a sanitarium under the care of a psychiatrist who could do no more than apply a poultice of polysyllables to a wound he could neither see nor understand any better than the next man, Greta came home and, shortly thereafter, succeeded in the act on which she had resolved. This time she made sure her departure was swift and certain.

There was nowhere to look but into my daughter's blue eyes, from which she managed to withhold whatever she may have thought or felt, in the tradition of childhood. No one seems to know whether that vacancy is innocence or guile. No one can seem to remember from his own childhood. We walked in dreams of sunsets, looking for violets and daisies beside the road, cutting switches to flick in the summer air, watching sparrows dip among the dusty reeds, greeting neighbors. Once we saw Mrs. Grundy coming toward us. We agreed she was one of those people who always ask you whether you're doing what you're doing. "Mowing the lawn?" "Shining the car?" "Doing your Saturday shopping?" In whispers we hastily anticipated Mrs. Grundy's greeting: "Out walking together?" It was so accurate that when Mrs. Grundy was again out of earshot, Carol shook her head deploringly and said, "We really shouldn't make fun of her. She always gives us kids things when we play around her house." The girl's impish streak was clear but had its limits; it stopped short of those to whom she was loyal or who were loyal to her. Thus she took exception to the boy in second grade who explained that he had put a wad of chewing gum on the teacher's chair "because it doesn't hurt as much as a tack," not because of the *non sequitur* in the testimony which delighted a grownup, but because she liked the teacher more than she did the boy.

I took Carol on my knee one day and said, "I'd like to move a little farther out into the country. How would you like that?" She didn't like it too well, but she didn't object either, no doubt understanding her father's wish to leave town. Mrs. Brodhag came along, after ascertaining that the house I bought was near a Congregational church. The human mechanism was breaking down everywhere, she said, and it was time we all began worshiping our Maker.

As we left town behind the truck carrying our furniture, we passed the house of the man who had lost the hyacinthine-haired boy. He was standing in the front yard, and I waved as we went by, but he didn't see me. He was in the middle of the lawn, looking up, with his hand over his mouth, as though he had been surprised by something in the summer sky. I wanted then to stop the car and rush back and tell him what nonsense I knew it had been to remind him that he had three other children. But of course I never did, and as we lurched past the van loaded with our belongings I looked straight ahead, refraining from any further sight-seeing until we were out of this town and heading through open country toward our new one, a scant fifteen miles away. Before we reached it, Carol fell asleep with her favorite doll in her arm, a circumstance of which Mrs. Brodhag, who was riding with us in the front seat, took advantage by gathering the girl in her own sturdy arm and, in gentle tones, resuming her sermon concerning the need for human faith.

eleven

THE WORLD POSED itself for the time being as a New Neighborhood rather than a teleological riddle, solvable or otherwise, and I saw ours through Carol's eyes, not Mrs. Brodhag's or even my own. The house was a colonial cottage with original beams and a pitch to its floors scarcely less acute than that of the back lawn, down which, the first thing I knew, Carol was tumbling with a playmate named Pidgie Harris. The two of them rolled side over side down its grassy slope, reciting the Pledge of Allegiance. Pidgie was our first overnight guest, and my next most incisive picture of those days is of the two of them playing a game called Hanging Down, which I believe they invented. You are put to bed but don't want to sleep, so you hang over the sides of the bed like bats and look at each other from underneath it. The first one to get dizzy loses.

"Aren't you tired yet, girls?"

"What time is it?"

"Nine o'clock."

"No, not yet."

That thirst for the suspension of logic which children supply was well slaked by that pair! One night, shortly before a Saturday on which I had promised to take them in to the Planetarium, they hustled me out of my armchair for a study of the stars. When asked why a lecture on the heavens was so urgent, they said, "So we'll understand the Planetarium when we go there." Pidgie's father had been to Europe, Asia, and Minnesota, her mother was half Republican, and I don't know what all. Pidgie was physically more suited than Carol to the pastime known as Teapot, which consists in pantomimic recital of the rhyme:

> I'm a little teapot, short and stout,
> Here's my handle [right hand on hip],
>   here's my spout [left hand so poised];
> When I get all steamed up, hear me shout,
> Just tip me over and pour me out!

The tableau dissolves as the child collapses in hysterics on the ground, or the tortured bed.

Pidgie was lost where found — in school. Just before the girls passed into third grade, rezoning took her out of Carol's school into another, and though she stayed in town she vanished from our orbit as completely as if she had left. That was just as she was on the verge of snaring Carol for the Episcopal church, where you "curtsy before you sit down." Any countercampaign would have been for Mrs. Brodhag to wage, my indifference to where Carol spent Sunday mornings (that is to say, my refusal to be bigoted about it) being responsible for my letting Mrs. Brodhag take her to the Congregationalists' Sunday school. Of the single year in which she went, I remember two things chiefly. One was a Thanksgiving dinner enlivened by Mrs. Brodhag's inclination to say grace. Having said it (she took most of her meals with us), she flapped out her napkin, and in a tone combining piety with the encouraging heartiness of a Girl Scout leader, said, "Now then! What have we to be thankful for?"

"That we're not Pilgrims" was Carol's unhesitating reply.

The other incident occurred during the Christmas holidays on an occasion when I was not present. In Sunday school, Carol created a mild crisis by her wish to include eight reindeer in the Nativity crèche, to which they had all been invited to contribute animals. She was indulged by the Sunday school teacher, who, I am sure, must have removed them later. Even so, the liberality made me wonder with a smile what my Sunday school teachers in bygone Chicago would have thought of this brand of improvisation. Any such Creative Play would have been given short shrift, I fear, with a rap on the head with a hymnal to boot.

I was not coaxed into the house of God until Christmas afternoon, when Carol's class appeared in the course of the Candlelight Service to sing "Go Tell It on the Mountain." The cherubs fluting in their white robes of the birth of Our Lord, seen elsewhere dragging his Cross in stained glass or ascending to heaven amid clouds of glory; the smell of the church (that dim spicy pungency common to all churches and constituting, quite literally, the odor of sanctity) evoking almost more than the music the lost songs of my own childhood; the blue eyes of my daughter catching mine for a moment before returning shyly, and rather guiltily, to the conductor — all these things mingled into one aching jumble that touched the very nerve of nostalgia. Memories of flowerless services and grim interrogations in catechism class, of Sunday afternoons at home wreathed with the smells of coffee and of cigars brandished by uncles locked in eternal dispute, of Old World women, their fat knuckles wound in handkerchiefs soaked in cologne, listening respectfully while their menfolk gave each other chapter and verse, all returned to me now. These memories were like flowers themselves, long hidden in corners of my heart, made suddenly to unfold their petals and yield their essences in a white New England meetinghouse so far in space and spirit from the church in whose shadow I had lived my boyhood. "Too bad you don't have more feeling for those things," Mrs. Brodhag would again say! And I twisting in my pew while every known emotion blazed within me. I thanked God when, propelled by a last, deranging squall of organ music into the winter twilight, I felt the cold air on my cheeks and my daughter's warm hand in mine.

Going to the bowling alley together was rather better. Mrs. Brodhag usually came along, if I shouldn't again say it was we who accompanied her. She was equally a crusader for this bodily exercise, and had discovered Claney's Lanes on the West Highway. We visited them, the three of us, almost every Friday night for a long time during the year Carol turned eleven. I encouraged this incorporation of Mrs. Brodhag into the family out of a feeling that Carol should be supplied some substitute for a maternal influence. Even after this passage of time, there was little sign that she would be acquiring a mother more formally.

That partial solitude in which I saw one year pass into another was often acute, but not enough so to bring to imprudent fruition any of the few companionships I did contract in my rather limited social rounds — attachments that would have entailed in each case, at any rate, complications as great as my own. And, too, there was always a portion of my emotions assigned to Greta; a high fee exacted for all memories of our happy times, of which there had been many, and possessing an intensity all the more to be prized for the troubles with which they had been intermixed.

There is something about a bowling alley that is marvelously invigorating, quite apart from the physical exercise. The continual reverberation of the pins is tonic in itself. It stirs the blood, wakes up sluggish corners of the nervous system, puts one into a new element. Being plunged with others into a world of pure muscular revel, of hurled balls and shattered targets contributing one's own thunderclaps to the orgy of racket, of hotdogs and beer and gleaming wood and metal — all are part of the intoxication of the public bowling alley. I found the pastime a sure way of "forgetting," of worming myself of nerves and misery, of discharging long days of static melancholy and boredom and regret.

I was fair, Mrs. Brodhag was good, and Carol — she was in a class by herself. She had originally come along only to watch, but for her that was impossible. Everything was a challenge: the piano, the bicycle, the choir, dancing, roller skating, ice skating — and now that black ball propelled not only by grownups but by slips of girls like herself, girls of fourteen and twelve, so why not a girl of ten, going on eleven?

The spectacle of her taking her turn was something to behold. The ball, even the children's weight, was almost too heavy for her, but she carried it in two hands to the foul line. There she would drop it with just enough force to send it on a ride the length of the alley. It took quite a while to complete its journey, and she would stand there waiting patiently, shifting from one foot to the other as she watched, sometimes inclining her head to one side in a way that dropped all her gold hair onto one shoulder. Sometimes, resting an elbow on a palm, she would lay her hand against her cheek, waiting. With just enough momentum to roll the last few inches, the ball would sort of jostle the pins aside, rather than knock them down, but over they would go, here one, there two or three. Sometimes players in neighboring alleys would pause to watch too, smiling. In this fashion she often got a spare, several times a strike, and, one evening, a score of a hundred and sixty-two.

twelve

I ONCE SPENT an evening with several companions in the last brandied hours of which we got to debating the question, "What is the greatest experience open to man?" There we sat trading anecdotes like fictional clubmen, not too inappropriately since we encircled a corner table in the lounge of the Gotham Club, where we had dined, eight strong, as guests of Frank Beerwagon, to celebrate his accession to power at the agency for which we all worked.

The topic is one of those conducive to everything but conclusion. There was no want of diversity in the answers that night. Of course there were the usual depositions for fleshly ecstasy. George Winrod favored us with a reminiscence of an Eastern queen possessing talons so long she could have torn the flesh from your back with a slash, but with which she bestowed, instead, extraordinary caresses. Andy Biddle recalled a select Neapolitan wallow where till morning . . . Kimberly, breathing smoke, broke in on this poppycock to remind us that the highest human experiences were not sensations but emotions. Since the mystic raptures of the saints must be a closed book to a company so minded, he went on, with a sardonic glance around it, and the same probably went for those next in glory, the aesthetic ones of the poets, we must be content with comparing notes in the more mundane scale of episodes. "I have no doubt this is one of the great nights of Frank's life," he said, with a flourish of his cigar at our host. "Not a peak of ecstasy, but a rich, deep-down happiness. Eh, Frank?"

This was for Beerwagon himself to say. Tapping an inch of ash from his own cigar, he smiled and allowed that it was certainly *one* of the climaxes of his existence. The only thing that topped it that he could think of was the night, eleven years ago, when he had nearly perished in the drifts of a mid-Nebraska blizzard but survived to tell it. Tell it, of course, he did.

"I was driving home for my sister's wedding, and believe you me, I thought they were going to get a funeral thrown in with it," he began. "The snow was just *dumped* out of the sky. I had to abandon my car in a foot of it before I knew it had started, and make my way toward the lights of a — well, I thought it was a house till it turned out to be a trailer truck, also abandoned. No haven or refuge in a blizzard, because it happened to be a refrigerator truck hauling dressed beef from Omaha." Here a snicker from Andy Biddle imperiled a pregnant pause in what was, after all, a quest for the sublime. The rest of us knew better where our bread was buttered, or to put it more fairly, had nervous systems slightly stabler than that possessed by the poor devil who had just demonstrated the reverse of his failure to laugh at the Boss's jokes. "Go on, Frank," said Kimberly softly.

"Well, sir, I like to never reached a decision what to do," continued Frank, who enjoyed throwing in reminders of his Midwestern roots now that he had made the grade in the East. "To stay in my car or in the cabin of the truck might have meant freezing to death. Legging it toward town with no precise knowledge where the nearest human habitation was might have meant meeting the same end in a ditch. It was now dusk, and I could see nothing — nothing but white. I remembered from a sign I'd just passed that I was inside some town limits. How close to the town proper? Well, the driver of the truck must have thought or known he was close to houses, or a gas station or something, so I decided to follow in his footsteps. Don't take that literally, my hearties, because they were now obliterated. I set out with an apprehension that soon became fear, and then panic. I floundered in drifts to my waist. My eyes were plastered shut by flakes like wet goose feathers. A wind howled in my ears — which, incidentally, began to freeze. I had no earmuffs. Darkness descended."

We sat forward on the edges of our chairs, except for the luckless Andy Biddle, who, head in hand, was trying to conceal the effect on him of the image of his lord slogging through an Alpine hell *sans* earmuffs. Or perhaps he was still thinking of those beeves hanging in the trailer, which the raconteur had bade fair to resemble by morning, to hear him tell it.

"Then just as I was sure it was only a question now of *how* I would go — collapse or freeze — I saw — only a few feet ahead since that was as far as you could see in that howling waste — the lights of a farmhouse. My sensation as I stumbled over that cottage threshold, wet, blind, and deaf — "

Here poor Andy Biddle gave way. The squeal strained through a mouthful of handkerchief told us that his days with the firm were numbered. We watched him draw the cloth from that troubled aperture like a conjurer performing an act of legerdemain. Oh, he was through, all right! A chill had fallen on Beerwagon's narrative of his most memorable experience, but he concluded it with dignity.

"My sensation as I stumbled into that warm kitchen can be imagined by any sensitive person. Yes, I can honestly call that the greatest moment of my life."

In the silence we now watched Kimberly nibble a single nut in thought. It would be a pity if this adventure did not meet his standards as posed in the brief remarks that had preceded it.

"You see, Frank, I disagree with you that it was a sensation you experienced. It was an emotion. But even if it was a sensation," Kimberly continued, exacting the maximum in office politics from the demurrer by turning to some of the others as he added, "it was not a mere animal pleasure. I would even venture to call that experience mystical, Frank. No, I won't take that back. It was mystical. You were restored to the human race. You were Saved."

And on that sublime note the evening ended.

Next morning Frank Beerwagon dropped into my office to apologize. "Whatever for?" I asked in genuine bafflement. Because I, alone, had not been given a chance to relate my most unforgettable experience. I told him to forget it, and that, come to think of it,

Kimberly hadn't really obliged either. He had contributed a brief homily laying down standards for the rest to meet, but on any illustrative private anecdote, he had fudged. "Hmm, you're right," said Frank, taking his thoughtful leave.

I should have fudged too. I should have been frankly stumped for a nomination from my private life. Because of this, I continued for some days to mull over the precise significance of the question as I reviewed the evening itself. There had been what critics always call, in reviews of anthologies, a few notable omissions. Nobody had cited his wedding night as the pinnacle of experience, perhaps because of an unwritten agreement to keep wives out of these stag affairs. Why had Kimberly not mentioned his having been aboard the *Andrea Doria* the night she collided with the *Stockholm?* Undoubtedly, because it might have topped the Boss's contribution to the literature of escape. Included in that literature must surely be George Winrod's recent realization that he had not, after all, gotten a certain office secretary in trouble. The bliss of deliverance from that hell I knew damn well to have exceeded the pleasure that had precipitated him into it, or even any the Burma girl with the red claws could have conferred. On a par with the Boss's story, as far as having that convincing ring was concerned, had been only Fred McQuarrie's account of his rescue from a foxhole on Iwo Jima.

I made a tentative conclusion. It seemed from all of this that uppermost among human joys is the negative one of restoration: not going to the stars, but learning that one may stay where one is. It was shortly after the evening in question that I had a taste of that truth on a scale that enabled me to put my finger on the specific moral for which we had, in all our rambling camaraderie, been groping.

My daughter Carol, then eleven, fell ill. An undulating but persistent temperature, pains in her back that recurred like the fever, in time ruled out the flu, for which the doctor has dosed her with the antibiotics that are the profession's first fusillade at whatever puts anybody to bed in the winter nowadays. This was in the late winter, around the middle of March. The trouble continued, with enough letups for nothing conclusive to have been thought or done by early April. Then Dr. Cameron, pulling a jowl over the back pains, which now seemed focused in the lower spine, hospitalized Carol "for X ray and so on."

My heart sank at the specters that raised their heads. Rheumatic fever, crippling arthritis . . . This was a dream of a child. Hair like cornsilk, blue bird's-wings eyes, and a carriage that completed the resemblance to a fairy sprite. One would not have been surprised to see her take off and fly away in a glimmer of unsuspected wings.

The week in the hospital was a long and exquisitely serialized course of suspense. Nothing in the X ray, nothing in the blood tests, nothing in the other examinations. There remained a report on a throat culture that had had to be sent to the state laboratory. That turned up some streptococcus infection.

"So that's it," Dr. Cameron said, greeting me at the elevator. "Her temperature's been normal now for two days, so it's probably let up. She's just walked in the hall without any pains. She feels a lot better. Give it another day and you can take her home. But anyhow, we've eliminated everything serious."

That was the happiest moment of my life. Or the next several days were the happiest days of my life. The fairy would not become a gnome. We could break bread in peace again, my child and I. The greatest experience open to man then is the recovery of the commonplace. Coffee in the morning and whiskeys in the evening again without fear. Books to read without that shadow falling across the page. Carol curled up with one in her chair and I in mine. And the bliss of finishing off an evening with a game of rummy and a mug of cocoa together. And how good again to sail into Tony's midtown bar, with its sparkling glasses, hitherto scarcely noticed, ready to tilt us into evening, the clean knives standing upended in their crocks of cheese at the immaculate stroke of five. My keyed-up senses got everything: the echo of wood smoke in Cheddar, of the seahorse in the human spine (the fairy would not be a gnome!), of the dogwood flower in the blades of an electric fan, or vice versa . . . But you can multiply for yourself the list of pleasures to be extorted from Simple Things when the world has once again been restored to you.

I threw myself into my neglected correspondence, which included a request from the editors of my college paper for a brief statement of my philosophy of life. They wanted to publish it as one of a series of such credos from representative alumni. I fell with gusto to the drafting of a basic belief in two hundred words or less:

"I believe that man must learn to live without those consolations called religious, which his own intelligence must by now have told him belong to the childhood of the race. Philosophy can really give us nothing permanent to believe either; it is too rich in answers, each canceling out the rest. The quest for Meaning is foredoomed. Human life 'means' nothing. But that is not to say that it is not worth living. What does a Debussy *Arabesque* 'mean,' or a rainbow or a rose? A man delights in all of these, knowing himself to be no more — a wisp of music and a haze of dreams dissolving against the sun. Man has only his own two feet to stand on, his own human trinity to see him through: Reason, Courage, and Grace. And the first plus the second equals the third."

Having dispatched this manifesto to the editors who had requested it, I flew with Carol for a few days' vacation in Bermuda. There we basked among the bougainvillaea blossoms and dodged motor scooters and watched the lizards on the patio wall. One afternoon as we sat in the sun I noticed that Carol's pleasure in these things was waning. She sat with her head against her hand, the postcard she had been composing to a friend back home fallen to the ground, and when I asked her what was wrong she complained of being tired and hot. I got a local doctor, who found her temperature to be a hundred and two and dosed her with another round of antibiotics. We flew back the next day, by which time the back pains had revived, and when we got home I realized how hollow her cheeks were and how waxen her color. Dr. Cameron's next blood test was more fruitful than the others. It showed an elevated white count.

"I'll tell you what I'd like to do," he said. "I'd like to take a bone marrow specimen."

"No . . . "

"Nonsense. There's any number of things we make this test for. There's — " And he proceeded to enumerate everything except the disease whose name had sprung into my mind.

I had to carry Carol to the car for this trip to the hospital. The conviction that one was being systematically tortured revived with the report from Dr. Cameron that the pathologist making the aspiration had used a syringe not precisely dry, vitiating the specimen. We went back the next day, with Carol in such discomfort that Mrs. Brodhag came along to hold the girl's head in her lap and soothe her brow, while she told her stories and jokes. That evening we were rewarded with a telephone call from Dr. Cameron saying that he had been in touch with the pathologist and would be over directly with the report.

Mrs. Brodhag monkeyed about in her kitchen, from a window of which she could see the doctor drive up. She told me later she knew what he had to say from the way he sat in his car a moment before getting out, giving his coat collar a kind of adjustment. He entered the house swinging his bag, somewhat like a hammer thrower in a weight contest preparing to see how far he could hurl it, and he smiled as he marched upstairs first to see the patient. I waited in the living room with my hand locked around a glass of whiskey. When he returned, shouting bluff instructions about dropping those coloring books and keeping up with our homework, he noticed Mrs. Brodhag still hanging about. He dispatched her on some sickroom errand or other that left the two of us together. He hesitated a moment, giving some such flirt to his coat lapels as Mrs. Brodhag must have noted, but at last spoke the word whose utterance could no longer be postponed. We both remained standing for the verdict.

"Baxter and I have been going over these slides at the hospital," he said, his voice slowing as he neared the name on which I knew now I was to be skewered, "and there seems to be a strong suggestion of leukemia."

The future is a thing of the past. I still fancy that that was what went through my mind then, precisely in those words, though they were a remark of Stein's, whom I was not to meet till a week later — "on the barricades," as he called the parental get-togethers in the Children's Pavilion at Westminster Hospital.

"Fix me one of those, would you? . . . Thanks . . . Now here's the thing. We have the world's leading authorities on its childhood forms right here in New York. You will take her in to Dr. Scoville tomorrow — "

"Can they do anything for it?"

"My dear boy, where have you been the last ten years? There are first of all the steroids — cortisone and ACTH — which give a quick remission. The minute she's pulled back to normal with those, Dr. Scoville will switch her to the first of the long-range drugs, some of which he's helped develop himself. If they should wear off, there's — but let's cross those bridges when we come to them." Dr. Cameron cleared his throat in the emphatic manner of one too busy to concern himself with matters that far in the future. "Now the first thing is to see that Carol does her homework so she'll pass into sixth grade without any hitch. Business as usual, that's the ticket. There isn't so much of the school year left that you can't help her through, but if you want, the town will furnish a tutor. Mrs. Quentin is excellent and won't talk. She won't even ask any questions."

"How long do these remissions last?"

The doctor described a circle so large the ice cubes rattled in his glass. "Years . . . "

"And by that time — "

"Of course! They're working on it day and night, and they're bound to get it soon." He jerked his head toward where he knew the telephone to be, and with an almost barroom-buddy solemnity said, "Chances are when I call Scoville to make an appointment for you he won't be home but at the laboratory with his rats. Oh, they'll get it! It's only a question of time, and that we've got on our side. As I say, ten years ago, nothing. Now a great deal. Look. Get this picture firmly fixed in your mind to the exclusion of everything else: *Carol going off to school again next September*. I promise it on my solemn oath."

We stood side by side at the window, where he paused a moment to distill if possible a greater degree of optimism between us, hitting thereby upon a tender little irony which he hoped would please me as much as it did him.

"When she graduates from junior high, you'll still be a worried father." He took a copious pull on his drink and gestured toward the playground at the bottom of the yard on which the view here gave. "You might make sure those swings and things are in good working order. And the porch of that playhouse looks a little rickety to me. Have a carpenter check it if you're not a do-it-yourself man. After all, we don't want anything to happen to our girl," he said, and, turning, gave me a shy, almost boyish smile, as though he were offering me the key to courage.

thirteen

DR. SCOVILLE was standing at his desk in a white
hospital coat drying his hands on a paper towel when I
entered his office on the fourth floor of the Westminster
Hospital. He was an old thirty-five or a young fifty, it
was hard to tell. Too much window sunlight bathed a
face too recently burned in some three-day medical
conference at a Southern seaside resort, and wreathed,
just then, in a smile of greeting which converted both
lines and color into what one suspected to be a carica-
ture. There was a thatch of gray hair, but it was crew-
cut. He discarded the towel and extended one of the
hands with which he had just examined Carol in an
anteroom separated from the consulting room by thick
walls and closed doors. Toils reported to be unflagging
had bent his shoulders into a stoop that, however, the
nature and persistence of his smile caused to appear
servile. It was a shopkeeper's smile. But at the same time
the apologetic and disclaiming smile of one who begged
you to remember that he was not the owner but only
worked here. The smile of a man who knew that every-

one who came through that door would be short-weighted.

"The spleen is beginning to be felt, so the disease is coming along," he said, when we had both sat down. "Her hemoglobin is" — he consulted a paper a receptionist had put on his desk — "just a thousand. Down almost three hundred from the test Dr. Cameron ran Tuesday. So things are getting touch-and-go."

He laced his hands behind his head and blinked into the sunlight a moment.

"The two best drugs we have for acute leukemia are 6-mercaptopurine and Methotrexate. I'd like to start her on the 6-MP, but it needs a few weeks to take hold, and I don't know whether we have the time. She's pretty explosive. But let's try it. If things get tricky we'll just pop her into the hospital and dose her with cortisone. We like to keep the steroids for later, an ace in the hole, but if we need them now to pull her into shape for the 6-MP, we'll have to use them."

"What do you mean by things getting tricky?"

"Watch her for bleeding. What the disease does is destroy the platelets in the blood, which do our clotting for us. It's important she doesn't fall down or bump or cut herself in any way. No playgrounds or such till we get her into remission. If she goes to school, no gym, and tell the teacher to watch her."

"What shall I tell the teacher she has?"

"Say it's anemia. Tell Carol the same thing. That's part of it, after all. Why not keep her out of school till we're over the hump? I'll give you some 6-MP to start her on, and we'll keep our fingers crossed. If she springs a nosebleed, pack it tight with this hemostatic yarn I'll give you. If it doesn't stop, shoot her into the hospital and we'll put her on the steroids."

"How long do the remissions last?"

"From the steroids, not long. From the other two drugs, anywhere from six months to a year or two. It's impossible to predict. About fifty per cent respond to the drugs."

"There are no cures?"

He smiled very tenderly across the desk. "That depends what you mean by a cure. I have a girl, now fifteen, who's been in the clear on 6-MP for over three years now. I'm sure in the end the cancer cells will develop a resistance to the drug."

"And then you'll switch to Methotrexate."

"And then we'll switch to Methotrexate."

"And by that time . . . "

"We hope so! Chemotheraphy — drugs — is the scent we're on now, and it's only a few years ago we didn't have anything at all. It's quite a game of wits we're playing with this beast. The 6-MP, for example, breaks the cells up nutritionally by giving them counterfeit doses of the purine they like to gorge themselves on. I hope we'll have some other pranks to play on him soon, and if there are, you may be sure the clinic downstairs will be the first to try them out. There's nothing hot at the moment, but who knows? It's an exciting chase, though I can't expect you to look at it that way at the moment."

"Do you believe in God as well as play at him?"

"Between my work at the clinic and tearing around to every other hospital in the country, I sometimes go for weeks without seeing my own children. I have no time to think about such matters. Now when I take you downstairs to the clinic, where we'll see Carol from now on, I think we'd better run another bone marrow. As you probably know, that's where blood is manufactured and where the villain's headquarters are. We'll only trouble her for a specimen every few weeks, once she's stabilized. I think we'll make a date to see her there on Monday."

We were destined to return to Westminster before that. On Sunday evening, a nosebleed the packing wouldn't stop sent us down the Parkway into New York at eighty miles an hour. In the back seat, Mrs. Brodhag kept the patient quiet with the game they had been playing all afternoon.

"My uncle has a grocery store," she said as we swept on through pouring rain, "and in it he sells — C."

"Carrots," I said.

"Oh, for heaven's sake, would I give anything that easy? And you keep your two cents out of it. Carol?" she prompted the girl nestled in her sturdy arm.

"Clorox," said Carol, who was on to the woman's trick of stocking her uncle's grocery store with everything but groceries. "Say, I believe it's stopped. Why do we have to go to the hospital now, Daddy?"

"Just to humor me. If it's really stopped I'd rather they took the packs out at the hospital anyway. Let's get on with the game. Is it cookies, Mrs. Brodhag? If not, I give up."

We had both given up by New Rochelle, where Mrs. Brodhag told us the terrible news. It was kohlrabi her uncle sold, which sent father and daughter into fits of choked laughter. By the time we had reached the city, the rain had stopped. Carol was promptly put to bed in the hospital, where a transfusion was begun and the first of the cortisone prescribed by a young doctor who had been in touch with Scoville, and who assured me we would have her out of there in a few days. Mrs. Brodhag and I walked down the hospital steps to the parked car, beside which we hesitated a moment as Mrs. Brodhag cast her eye up the dark street. I looked for a restaurant.

"Would you like a bite to eat?" I asked, for we had had no supper.

She shook her head, fixing her gaze on a building halfway up the block which I saw to be a church. Sensing her wish, I offered to wait and even to loiter with her there a moment. I expressed doubts as to the suitability of the building we approached, for it bore the name of St. Catherine of Siena and was surmounted by a cross, whereas my friend was a Congregationalist habituated to plain interiors and spare devotionals. "This will have to do," she said as we entered all that splendor.

She knelt at the front to pray. I sat in a pew toward the middle. The silent cavern had at this late hour only a sprinkling of bowed heads. Mrs. Brodhag was a long time, and I rose and drifted to the back of the church, where my attention was caught by a separate small bank of trembling candles and a statue they dimly illumined. It was a shrine to St. Jude, the Patron of Hopeless Cases. I sank to the floor and, squeezing wet eyes to hands clenched into one fist, uttered the single cry, "No!"

I now mastered the art of remaining half drunk while having lost the joy of drink. Alcohol and barbiturates between them afforded a few hours of tumbling dreams, like those somersaults of men pictured in space fantasies as floating beyond the gravity of any world, life or death.

One awoke from nightmares to a nightmare. Daybreak brought its jumble of bird songs that had once vouch-safed the happy dozer a fancy of inhabiting dense jungle, a game doubly available to those ignorant of the names of the creatures fluting away out there. But one bird we knew, that brown thrush with the sweetest sound on earth, if it is not the most unbearable. One nested near the house this season, spilling its liquid music among the cruel May boughs. I must have heard him in my sleep, for I awoke with the tears leaking from sealed lids.

I was glad to get to the hospital, where the corridor was as full of children as the woods had been of birds. I had seen it only in the ghostly gloom of midnight. Now it was a bedlam of colliding tricycles, bouncing balls, and shouts for nurses and the volunteer workers known as Bluejays, so named for the color of the uniforms in which they bustled about on nonmedical errands. A Negro nurse clutching a pan covered with a towel was with her free hand holding at bay a boy in pajamas who was trying to use her stomach for a punching bag. She was laughing uproariously. A mother wheeling a per-ambulator in which reposed a mummy with a sign pinned to its gown reading "Nothing by mouth" paused to smile at the scene. A priest blessed a lad in a wheel chair before trading taunts with him about the Dodgers as he moved off to other chores. Crawling toward us on all fours was an infant wearing a turban of surgical gauze, whom a passing nurse snatched up and returned to its crib.

Carol's room was empty. The unoccupied bed was cranked up, and on the table beside it lay the storybook we had taken from home, closed, with a stick of gum for a marker. A nurse entering just then with some medication thought we might have better luck in the playroom. That was where she was, sitting in a wheel chair, working at a coloring book with one hand. High on a pole affixed to the chair dangled a bottle from which a thin tube of crimson led to a needle in her other hand, and there was no doubt its influence had already spread to her cheeks. Her bright "Hi" happily confirmed the impression, though its tone of welcome soon dissolved into one of complaint. There were a number of things, one major. Some "society lady" had braided her hair into pigtails, which were both libelous in effect and ruinous to the waves she was trying to cultivate. I complied instantly with the order to remove the rubber bands, and brushing the precious fleece, I asked why she had submitted. "What can you *do*, Daddy? They have this *attitude*."

"What attitude?" I whispered.

She lowered her voice further and indicated with her eyes the Bluejay whose efforts I was unraveling. "Watch her a while."

The volunteer was a slender brunette of thirty or so whose own grooming, triumphant over uniforms, and rippling assurance testified to a lifetime of security, of swimming pools and tennis matches in expensive club sunlight and charity balls under great chandeliers. She was clapping her hands over a colored boy who lay on a wheel table narrating his surgery in tones of frightened bravado. He too wore a turban, through whose cerements the deleted lump could be seen slowly rising again, like a brioche in a pan. "Oh, that's wonderful, Tommy. What all you'll have to tell the kids when you go home!"

The Bluejay moved from child to child, spooning food

into the mouths of laggard breakfasters, adjusting a television set before which sat a small group in a vinework of transfusion and intravenous tubes, getting out games and puzzles for those at tables. By the time she circled back to us I had thoroughly dismantled her handiwork. She paused over us to take it in.

"*Look*," she cried with the ritual clap of delight. "How pretty."

"You like it?" I asked, looking up with a dog's eyes. My gaze was evidence that I thoroughly understood what Carol meant by "that attitude."

"Why, it's beautiful. How do you like to part it, dear, middle or side?"

"Side."

"That's perfect for you. So make sure Daddy does it right. Dad-*dy*," and she made off with a pedagogical scowl at me. She pretended to have forgotten the pigtails or had actually forgotten them, in adherence to that sacred hoax to which we were now one and all committed down to the gates of death: the hoax that Everything Was Fine.

This trust was hardest to uphold in the visitors' lounge, where parents, in respites from their vigils, found themselves comparing troubles in chats into which the subjects might at any moment walk or bolt in wheel chairs or tricycles. That was where I met Stein. I had just seen Carol settled in bed for an after-luncheon nap and had gone into the lounge for a cigarette. A short man with a bald bullet head, wearing a suit of brutal green, was standing at the window looking out. He turned around when I entered, and gave a snort of welcome.

"What are you in for?" he asked in a tone suggesting

that our communications be henceforth conducted as parodies of those between men unjustly imprisoned. I told him and asked what ailed his little one. "Same thing. They all got some form of it here. The infinite variety of Nature."

"How long has she had it? He or she?"

"Rachel. This is her first time in."

The job of describing his attitude as one of assertive hopelessness is nothing to that of portraying his effect on me, which was that of a repulsive man to whom I was instinctively drawn. He should better always face the world with his back, Stein, than have to turn around and show that face. Corners may be cut by evoking the snuffed outlines and aspiring tusks of a pug dog, although his nose was not blunted, but rather a small replica of the rocket bestowed on him for a head. He was Cerberus, welcoming newcomers to those infernal shades which they might never leave, whose exits he would bar as conscientiously as he greeted their arrivals. After a few moments of conversation he suddenly said, "Come here," and led the way through a glass door onto a roof terrace.

There through a grilled window we looked into a research laboratory filled with caged mice. An attendant was cleaning the cages and putting fresh food and water into the cups. To one side of another window, using the sill for a work counter, sat two technicians busy at a task. A girl was taking mice one at a time from a hamper and holding them while a man measured tumors on their undersides with a pair of calipers. Measurements were noted in a book, as was also the weight of the mouse, which was put on a scale before being chucked back into the hamper and another extracted for the same procedure.

Seeing they had an audience, the two scientists became grave and efficient, then changed this attitude into one of humor. They both began to laugh about something. In the midst of it all, a mouse got away and had to be retrieved. After this had been done, the girl reached down and for our benefit hilariously displayed a baited trap: they had mice! Stein and I strolled away eventually toward the roof's edge, where we stood at a parapet looking down into the street two floors below. A few hundred feet away, directly across from the research wing on whose edge we stood, was the church of St. Catherine.

"Quite a juxtaposition," I remarked. "Science versus religion."

Stein seemed to have been expecting this cliché, to have, in fact, been impatiently awaiting its utterance. The bitterness of his answer suggested that he may even have lured me out onto the terrace in order to feed him the line.

"We get about as much from the one as the other," he said with a snort that was a finely shaded variation of his welcome in the lounge. I had not been prepared for such a range of nuance in the human grunt.

"Oh, come now."

He shook his head. "They'll never get it, cancer. They'll never conquer it. Do you know what it is, that sluggishly multiplying anarchy? A souvenir from the primordial ooze. The original Chaos, without form and void. In de beginning was de void, and de void was vit God. Mustn't say de naughty void," he finished in a sudden spasm of burlesque that could only have revealed a man so full of hate that he is prepared to turn it on himself.

I was not without spirit of my own.

"I'd say that was a hell of a way to talk to a parent around here if I didn't remember why you were here yourself."

"Sorry." He laid a hand on my shoulder and led me back to the door. The Cerberus had better features of our lonely sojourn to suggest. "Had lunch? I found a swell bar and grill around the corner. Might as well get to know the points of interest."

To get to it we passed the church, and through the open doors I could glimpse the high altar and the muted blaze of rose and gold all around it.

"You don't believe in God," I said to Stein.

"God is a word banging around in the human nervous system. He exists about as much as Santa Claus."

"Santa Claus has had a tremendous influence, exist or not."

"For children."

"Lots of saints have died for God with a courage that's hardly childish."

"That's part of the horror. It's all a fantasy. It's all for nothing. A martyr giving his life, a criminal taking one. It's all the same to the All."

"I can't believe that."

"Congratulations."

We fell into a gloomy but curiously companionable silence. I changed the subject by jerking my head once more toward the research building before we turned the corner out of its sight. "We've got that to be grateful for, maybe even pious about. Ten years ago our children wouldn't have stood a chance."

"So death by leukemia is now a local instead of an express. Same run, only a few more stops. But that's medicine, the art of prolonging disease."

"Jesus," I said, with a laugh. "Why would anybody want to prolong it?"

"In order to postpone grief."

What enabled me to bear Stein's apothegms through the highly bibulous luncheon that followed was the knowledge, serenely hoarded, that I would have my sweet home in a day or two. The steroids for which solemn guarantees had been given were already surely hurling their magic against the foe. The assurance that the same was true of Stein and his Rachel helped me further through the interlude of chomping and snorting that passed for his noonday meal. Over his pilaf, he recalled a horse breathing into its oats. Of course he was enjoying himself; I was on to that. I had him taped. He was not pure intellect so much as a crock of soured emotions. I liked him.

Returning to our post of vigil we passed again the church of St. Catherine, this time on the other side of the street. From there could be read a bulletin announcing a novena to St. Jude a month hence. Several gray pigeons fluttered about the crucified figure over the central doorway.

"Have you ever noticed pigeons never soil that statue?" I said.

"Naturally the parish keeps it clean."

"No, I mean the birds themselves don't alight on it. Everywhere around it, but not there. Strange."

What else seemed strange was that Dr. Scoville never called that day nor the next. I was ready for words with him, but when I saw him enter the ward on the third afternoon he looked sixty years old, rumpled and unshaven, scarcely able to hold the dispatch case he was dragging in one hand. He had flown to five cities in a series of research conferences, with a dash to Washington to bludgeon loose some funds for an experimental drug costing fifteen thousand dollars a pound, and he had not slept in a bed, he told us cheerfully at the foot of Carol's, for thirty-six hours.

"Neither have I," said Carol, "with all the noise around here. It sounds like a *pet shop*."

Dr. Scoville raised her gown and studiously palpated her spleen. Not felt, his satisfied nod told me. The enemy had receded from that critical outpost. Nasal membrane still a bit friable but nothing to worry about, since the latest blood report showed the platelet count to be zooming back well up over a hundred thousand from a troublesome low of sixty-five thousand. And the roses in the cheeks told us all we needed to know about the hemoglobin. "Take her home tonight if you want."

She was dressed and ready with her valise long before I had paid the bill and was through the rest of the red tape of discharge. By that time the sun had set and a thunderstorm broken. Carol sprang down the stairs and into the car with squeals of laughter, and off we shot for the country and home.

"Will I be able to go to school tomorrow?"

"Of course! So when you get home, young lady, first thing you do is call your friends and get the homework you've missed. You've got to get back into the groove again, and no kidding."

"I wonder what Mrs. Brodhag will have for dinner."

"I talked to her on the telephone. Fried chicken and dumplings, mashed potatoes, and ice cream with hot fudge sauce. And for me, baby, a nice cold bottle of beer."

"Oh, Daddy, you and your beer! It's so *common*. Nobody drinks *beer*."

The burst of laughter had to be explained.

" 'Common' means that everybody does something, so if nobody does it, it's exclusive."

"Oh, Daddy, you're so *technical*. Anyway it sounds like a good dinner."

"What about a little party over the weekend? All the friends who've missed you. How would you like that? We'll discuss the whole thing with Mrs. Brodhag tonight."

Note on the doctrine of relativity: The happiest man in New York that night was a father heading for home through flashes of lightning and gusts of blinding rain, with a doomed child on the front seat beside him.

Stein was almost right but not quite. The future was a thing, not of the past, but of the present. Now began that time of living to the hilt, or of which one sometimes thought in terms of squeezing from each day what the frugal Mrs. Brodhag did from an orange — everything. I must make sure Carol missed absolutely nothing while giving no hint of this tormented aim. Nonchalance is called for in the unlikeliest places. Who would in all the labyrinth of parenthood ever have dreamed he would find frivolity a sacred trust?

First was a wish of mine to make Carol understand, and enjoy to the full, the exact texture of my bond with

Mrs. Brodhag. This involved going back to Mrs. Brodhag's first appearance at the house when Carol had been three and her father sick in bed as the New Woman walked in. She had been sent from the agency "on approval," and the green gaze turned on the man with the medicated cloth around his throat and the cocktail shaker full of fruit juice on the littered floor indicated just who would be approving whom. "I'll clean around you" were her first words.

With propped head I watched order brought out of chaos. The human woodchuck burrowing through disorder came at last to a book which had to be picked up off the floor and laid on a desk. Her frown when she paused to read its title suddenly recalled the agency woman's remark over the phone that the prospect had "once worked in a library."

"You don't like Mr. Hemingway?" I whispered from the bed.

For answer, she carried the volume gingerly between thumb and forefinger by a corner of its cover, so that its open pages hung down like the filthy rag it was judged to be.

Thus began that chain of literary criticism which so far as Mrs. Brodhag's end of it was concerned was conducted solely in pantomime. She seemed to accept the challenge of communicating exclusively in that vein, so that each author I "gave her" was an assignment for a charade. "What do you think of Thomas Wolfe?" I asked. She swung an imaginary mop about the floor: it was what he used for a pen. Faulkner? She wiped her feet of what could well be imagined in the barnyard evoked by the very name. I once mentioned a writer of popular novels more known for quantity than quality. Without hesitation she did this: She laid one hand alongside her nose, flung the other outward at arm's length, brought it back to her nose, and flung it out again, several times. This seemed to me as cryptic as some of the Higher Criticism, till I remembered the old-fashioned method by which yard goods were measured out by dry goods clerks. It was how the novelist turned the stuff out year after year, you see. Mrs. Brodhag had worked in a dry goods store as she had also a grocery store, before getting that part-time job in the local library. There the authorities had not been up to her graphic pronouncements, nor to her use of a "Grab-All" (the long-handled pincers with which things are taken down from upper shelves in grocery stores) on books. She was soon dismissed as too rich for everyone's blood.

Having filled Carol in on all these things that I had learned along the way, it remained for me to see that she got a demonstration of Mrs. Brodhag's technique. By now Mrs. Brodhag and I had reached a tacit agreement that we were playing a sort of game together, and that each artist I posed for her was a challenge to which to rise. I say artist because the field had widened to include painting, sculpture, music, and everything else aesthetic. One night I had a recording of Delius's *Sea Drift* going on the phonograph, and as Mrs. Brodhag, who always ate with us now, was clearing the dinner things away, I caught Carol's eye as if to say "Watch," and asked, "Mrs. Brodhag, what do you think of this?" The promptness with which she wrung out an imaginary handkerchief expressed an opinion all too long stored up: "sentimental slop" was her verdict on this choral work and on

Delius. She winked at Carol as she went out, in conspiracy of their having Daddy's number as to musical taste. I was delighted to see this for its great value in reaffirming for Carol the enfolding unity and integrity of the household. Imagine my surprise at having the whole thing blow up in my face.

"Why do you poke fun of her?" Carol asked me when I looked in on her as she sat reading in bed preparatory to going to sleep that night.

Had I expected too much or too little of childhood? Carol had not yet graduated from the forthright loves and mads and jealousies of little girls to the perceptive malices and flavored affections of maturity. Why try to force this bloom? Why try to make her more sophisticated than there might be time for? In place of the normal parent's wistful "Why must they grow up?", so recently mine too, was now the reverse: "How old will she get to be?"

I wasted no time clearing myself of the charge of patronage. I did not point out that I was a "fan" of Mrs. Brodhag's, that I thought her "wonderful" (that sorry tatter of sophistication). I simply said to the long lashes concealing from me the blue eyes bent to the book, "Oh, come now. The fact that we laugh at people doesn't mean we're making fun of them. You laughed at her in the car when she spelt 'kohlrabi' with a 'c.'"

The book was plunked face-down on the counterpane. "Oh, Daddy, you dope, she knows perfectly well how to spell 'kohlrabi.' We came across it a couple of days before in a book we were reading together. That's why she used it. She knew I knew it. It was just to add a little extra joke to that old game. So I laughed."

"Well, I'll be damned."

It was only by remarking that it was nine o'clock and time to put out the light that I recovered anything like the offensive.

"Well, that gives me another fifteen minutes. Because I'm bathed and in my nightgown."

"So?"

"So Mrs. Brodhag knows that takes fifteen minutes, so if I do it all beforehand, why, I get the extra time. Maybe it's time you started seeing her through *my* eyes."

I awoke her gently in the dusk of dawn.

"Have you ever seen a deer?"

She smiled and sleepily raised an arm to draw me down for what must be another of her voracious father's good-night kisses.

"I just saw one on the lawn," I whispered. "I think he's a young one."

I carried her into my bedroom, from the window of which I had a moment ago glanced out and glimpsed the dark shape moving past the hedge toward the woods beyond. Together we peered into the fresh gloom of morning. A late moon flooded the slope of grass, and a few stars were tangled in the old catalpa tree.

"There, isn't that him?" I said, pointing. "His head and antlers above the brush?"

"Oh, Daddy, you're probably seeing things."

"Well, no matter. We'll go to the zoo Saturday."

After the (as it turned out) false move in the Mrs. Brodhag business, I made a doubly conscientious effort to understand the precise tone and content of Carol's relation with her best friend, Omar Howard.

Omar was the oldest child in a neighbor family of numerous apple-eating sisters and brothers who had wandered down the road to Carol's house without profit or encouragement for years. Only Omar made any dent in her unwavering self-sufficiency and restrictive tastes. He had all the brains in the family and all the looks, though there was rather too much of him from the neck down. Plump cheeks stated a theme systematically repeated by a tummy which his parents, perhaps rightly, thought it amusing to encase in a Tattersall vest. Sitting with his thumb hooked in a pocket of it he recalled photographs of Henry James, whom he would certainly in later years read if he hadn't already — one put nothing past him. This Tom Thumb quality made him look a miniature version of a solid citizen. Being fourteen, he was in the local junior high, whose academic seams he was bursting, and on his way to prep school, Harvard, and God knew what all. He had been friends with Carol since a time when the two years' difference in their ages meant a lot more than it did now.

Instead of such a party as I had proposed, Carol just wanted Omar to dinner. After we'd had him, he called to ask Carol to a movie. His father did the chauffeuring in the family Chevrolet sedan, into the front seat of which the movie-goers had to crowd, the back being taken up with a wheelbarrow which Mr. Howard had bought secondhand somewhere, put in to drive home, and been unable to get out. Endless jimmying and juggling had failed, so far, to reverse its insertion. Now it was all impossibly twisted around, its position like a fetal "presentation" for Mr. Howard to contemplate, like an obstetrician contemplating a hopeless delivery. He was a bumbler of the first water who had enriched our domestic life more than he would ever know. Carol and I often saw him bouncing around town with his absurd burden behind him, its handles sometimes pointing back, sometimes nudging his neck, as they now did Omar's riding to the movie. Once we had driven past the Howard house and seen him in the driveway, scratching his head with his cap in his hand as through the open car door he pondered his puzzle for another try.

"They don't make them like they used to," I overheard Omar say as he and Carol came in the front door after the early show. He was a knowledgeable critic, being by virtue of television reruns able to achieve that connoisseurship of silent masterpieces and vanished comedians usually reserved for adult intellect. I heard Mr. Howard drive on, leaving Omar to walk home after a Coke with Carol. I rose from my living-room chair and asked about the picture. It had been terrible, as measured against, sure enough, a short composite of excerpts from the old comedies run as an extra feature. We were soon on the sacred subject of the thrown pie.

"And have you ever noticed, Daddy — Omar and I were just talking about it — have you ever noticed this," said Carol, shaking off her coat, "that after the one guy throws his pie and it's the other guy's turn, the first guy doesn't resist or make any effort to defend himself? *He just stands there and takes it.* He even *waits* for it, his face sort of ready? Then when he gets it, he still waits a second before wiping it out of his eyes, doing it deliberately, kind of solemn, as though the whole thing is a — "

"Ritual," said Omar. "You see it isn't a fight in the sense of something in which you defend yourself, but basically like your bullfight in Spain, where it isn't a sport either as we here think of it with our S.P.C.A. attitude — it's a *ceremony*. Even the way the face is wiped off is stylized, as Carol says. First slowly the eyes are dug out with tips of the fingers, then the fingers freed with a flip, then the rest of the face is wiped down strictly according to established rules . . . "

I hovered anxiously about while Carol fixed their refreshments in the kitchen. She was now puffed up as a result of the Meticorten. Its side effects were a colossal appetite plus a danger of high blood pressure requiring salt-free foods. The larder was stacked with dietetic canned goods and soft drinks which the ravenous girl by now loathed. There were periodic fits of rage, during which she screamed that she would take no more Meticorten if it meant eating the disgusting foods for which I scoured New York. I knew she had gorged herself on popcorn at the movie, and from the living room I could hear the hiss of forbidden bottle caps and the sound of the icebox being raided, but I hadn't the heart to make a scene in the presence of her friend. I retired, thankful this was the last week of the steroids.

It was a few days later that Mrs. Brodhag reported one of our best pieces of crystal missing. It was a Venetian goblet, of which I could hardly be expected not to make an issue. It had obviously been thrown out because it was broken. "I have a confession to make," Carol said at last. "Omar did it."

I laughed aloud, tucking this betrayal among my store of cute sayings with typical adult opacity. That evening

Omar phoned, but Carol was "not at home" to him. I thought this standard feminine caprice till the sight of her in tears in her room told another story. She didn't want him to see her in her present gross condition. "I'm as fat as — as he is!" she shouted, and picking up the box of Meticorten tablets hurled them against the wall.

Stooping to retrieve the scattered pearls, I remembered her and Omar a few years back in their more tender childhood, sitting on the doorstep making some serious effort to learn to snap their fingers; spelling words with their eyes closed, this obstacle being for some reason a special sporting condition; laughing over their first Saturday lunch in our kitchen as they sliced their bananas with scissors; gossiping about a local woman whose hair was "bleached black," etc., etc. — all the rest of the carefully noted cunning turns. There was the story she had written for an earlier grade beginning: "The cocktail guests were an ill, assorted group." The telegram she had sent me on my birthday, delivered over the same telephone from which it had been dispatched. Her habit of using "egghead" as an epithet for stupidity, synonymous with "knucklehead" or "pinhead," being unable in the crystalline domain of innocence to imagine a scale of values in which intelligence was suspect. I remembered her once accusing Omar of something by screwing a stiff finger into his stomach and saying, "Yours truly did it and nobody else."

Out of these disjointed reminders, like fire out of a jumble of brush, leaped the realization that she had not been betraying Omar at all by "confessing" that he had broken the Venetian glass. The gimmick word was indeed a measure of her loyalty: peaching on him was like peaching on herself.

As I gathered up the pearls I prayed, too, that the 6-MP, whose inauguration was scheduled for our next clinic visit, would be effective. But not too effective. It must destroy the villain without toxicity to the rest of the system. "Report any mouth sores, vomiting, or diarrhea immediately," Dr. Scoville instructed me when the campaign was finally launched.

For three weeks I sweated out the possible tragedy of a drug that could not be tolerated. I watched with crossed fingers while she sipped her breakfast orange juice, the acid test for inflamed gums. I telephoned in her first complaint with a sick heart — which the doctor freed like a bird from a snare by saying, "Fine, if it's no worse than that. That's where we like to keep them, on the edge of toxicity." Our luck held. When I took her back to the clinic, her weight was down, her blood normal. But a reviving villain reawakens in the marrow two weeks before there are any hematological signs that he is again stirring, so it was not until late that afternoon, when they telephoned the report on the sternal aspiration, that I knew we were in the clear.

"Can I take her on a vacation?" I asked, forcing my rapture from a throat still dry with fear.

"Anywhere. It's a solid remission. We won't need to see you for three weeks."

We flew to California, stopping off to visit my father as Carol herself had insisted. She had seen her grandfather three or four times before, in his strange habitat, and was ready for the sights and sounds that composed it. Indeed, I read in her wide eyes something of the

instinctive fascination of childhood with the phenomenon in question. She held my hand as the doors were
unlocked and the first of the inhabitants shuffled by us
along the corridor down which my father, rather his-
trionically, hobbled to greet us. A recent letter from the
doctor in charge, which I had shown Carol, prepared us
for the welcome.

"After he shakes my hand," the doctor had written,
"he always rubs his palm around the top of his head
three times, counterclockwise, which is an unusual thing
for a right-handed man. He ends up invariably by scratching the back of his head and his neck, and after com-
pleting this part of the procedure, he drums very rapidly
on top of his head with the other hand. Pathetic as it is,
it has its comical aspects, as I think you will agree, and
it also gives me something to think about, though, I
must admit, without much profit."

After the anticipated ritual, my father embraced his
granddaughter, whom he then swept into the lounge to
meet some of his friends. He insisted on holding her on
his knee for what, as he protested to me privately, might
be the last time. The flow of complaints soon started up,
threatening to bar the likelihood of poor Carol's ever
getting to meet his friends. But the friends, now semi-
formally queuing up for introduction, had to be presented. One was a beanpole of a youth in a denim shirt
who did nothing but grin. Another was a stocky, success-
ful-business-man type who after the greeting excused
himself on the ground that he was terribly busy. He
moved from chair to chair with a telephone ending in a
foot of frayed cord, for which he thanked an unseen
waiter, and over which he closed deals and barked at

subordinates in distant cities. The strangest of all was an old fellow who also did things on his bald dome with his hands. He would first place one hand flat on top of his head. Then he would smack the other on that, then withdraw the bottom one and place *it* on top, alternating this indefinitely for hours on end. The enthralled Carol finally asked him why he did that, and he answered, "If I don't, who will?"

Taking my father out for a walk, we passed the spot where I had proposed to Carol's mother long ago, as only I knew, who of course had never told her anything more than was necessary of her mother's past. At last it came time to return Grandpa to the ward, but before continuing on our holiday, I stepped alone into the doctor's office for a word with him. After a few comments about my father, chiefly the admission that there was nothing to be done for him, the doctor fidgeted in his swivel chair a bit and said abruptly, "How's the little girl?"

"What do you mean?"

"I noticed the sternal puncture. And the marks on her legs speak of recent Meticorten fat."

"She's on 6-MP."

"Working?"

"Great."

"And next there's Methotrexate, if you haven't played that card, and a new drug coming in from Germany, as well as the FUDR they're fiddling with clinically over here. Lots of things."

"Really?"

"Of course. Your doctor will no doubt tell you all about them in good time. In New York you're obviously at Westminster. Scoville, I suppose? World's leading authority on the acute."

"You know everything."

"God bless you both."

"You believe in Him?"

"And in man, which is a hell of a lot harder. Still there are times when we can, for which one is glad. Good-by."

"Good-by."

We flew to San Francisco, loved it, went by train to Los Angeles, and there our pleasure suddenly bogged down. We were sitting in our hotel bungalow across from the now *démodé* Brown Derby after a dreary day of sight-seeing, Carol brushing her hair in her bedroom and I sitting in mine hating myself for a father who knew nobody in Hollywood, but *nobody*, when I suddenly snapped my fingers and exclaimed, "Andy Biddle!" You remember the poor devil with the sense of humor that had made the Boss's gripping tales excruciating and his jokes flat? He had been sacked soon after the Big Dinner and promptly gotten a job in the publicity department of a major film studio. I knew the name of the hotel where he lived and had him on the phone in two minutes. In another thirty we were tumbling out of a cab in front of his place just outside Beverly Hills.

It was a perfect night for all three of us. Andy is one of those people who converse almost solely in anecdote, and he was at the top of his form. His endless, giggling yarns about the movie capital and people he knew there kept Carol in stitches. He told us this Hollywood story:

A prominent writer got a job in a studio where his first

assignment was a scenario of a best-selling novel about ancient Egypt, written by an inferior but far more popular author. He turned in his completed script and after five days or so was summoned into the producer's office. "This dialogue," said the livid producer. "It's laid in ancient Egypt and you've got characters saying things like 'Yes, siree.' What kind of talk is that for ancient Egypt?" The writer, a little puzzled, asked to see the passage in question and had the script fairly flung at him. He read the dialogue that was disturbing his superior, and found he had on his hands the task of explaining that the letters in question spelled, "Yes, sire."

Carol knew enough of costume pictures — princes throwing purses with exact amounts in them, glasses hurled into castle hearths — to get the point instantly. The curse of television! Laughter was merriest over the actor whose hand they made sure the dog would lick, as a sign of affection, by smearing beef gravy on his fingers before shooting the scene.

We came home by train, riding in a compartment but sleeping together in the lower, from which we peered out whispering and tittering at the midnight scenery. After the glimpse of Andy Biddle's life she taunted me with "Daddy, why don't you get a decent job?" How charming the way little girls hunch up their shoulders when they laugh, to which is often added the mannerism of inclining the head to one side, in shy apology for something brash just said or asked. Often as I lay with my grief in my arms, I thought of her mother, of whose body she had a more slender version, of whose face a purified form. With the effects of the Meticorten gone, the old poetic word "gracile" came once again to mind for the perfection, in motion or repose, of that compact roseflesh, firm in the bud. Enough has been said of the particular coloring, the honey and amber of hair and skin, to indicate that the yellow rose is meant rather than its pink sister.

She fell asleep, and as we pounded on through the continental night I tried to banish from my mind all thoughts but the single one: *She will go back to school.* She would push her bicycle up the long hill leading to it as usual, in order that she might coast down all the way home. Her hair would stream out behind her in a cloud of gold, and her legs would be outthrust above the whirling pedals, till the momentum had squandered itself against the upgrade leading into our drive, in which she would come to a perfectly timed stop just before the front door. I held this picture like a hoard of treasure as, breathing her fragrance about me, she turned over in my arm, jostling a few notes from a musical bear without which she would not think of going to bed. What had Cardinal Newman written in that loveliest of hymns? "I do not ask to see the distance scene; one step enough for me."

fourteen

SOLDIERS GOING into battle or embarking on missions of peril often reckon up their chances of coming out alive on the basis of odds that there is always some mathematician around to supply. Say twenty to one. Of this game there is a further refinement. Does luck in having emerged whole from previous dangers proportionately reduce the chances of doing so again? No, say the computers, the chances are the same each time: twenty to one.

Similarly does sickness make statisticians of us all, invokers of the laws of probability. When a relapsing marrow indicated that resistance had arisen to the first drug, and the beast after six months in chains was again abroad, the successor known as Methotrexate was hurled into the breach. It too had a fifty-fifty chance of being both effective and tolerable. Did luck with the 6-MP halve our odds on being lucky again? No, the average was the same. Indeed, the fact that the one drug worked indicated the second might.

The rise of the morbid cells in the marrow, which had

gone from twenty per cent to forty to fifty, was checked, slowly reversed — thirty per cent, fifteen, five, till at last a normal marrow was drawn from that breast bone to which the healers so remorselessly helped themselves. "We're back in business again," said Dr. Scoville, turning his old-boy smile on me like a revolving lighthouse beacon. Then he ran to catch a plane for London.

That spring my father died, and when I flew to Chicago I took Carol with me, not because I thought children should attend funerals, but in order not to spend a day away from her.

I loitered a moment among the nearby graves. Doc Berkenbosch was there now in that colony of the dead Dutch, as was old Reverend Van Scoyen, who had performed so well over Louie's deathbed — and of course Louie. On my mother's headstone were chiseled the words, "Awaiting the resurrection of Our Lord." Your husband never saw your grave, *Moeke*; he was too steeped in melancholy to mourn you at the time, and we never brought him down for the funeral. *Melancholie*, as your ancestral tongue has it. Here is a branch of early lilac, and for you I always liked the old Dutch word for long-suffering: *lankmoedig*. I drop it on your grave like a sprig of fadeless syllables. That reminds me of a bright saying of your granddaughter's. She once wrote a theme for school which had to be a character sketch of some member of the family, and hers began, "My long, suffering father . . . " Of course that was long ago and she laughs at it now, as she did at Andy Biddle's story of the Hollywood secretary whose typescript of a dictated story synopsis began, "This is a swash, buckling story . . . "

Vaarwel, lankmoedig moeder, vaarwell. Melancholiek vader, vaarwel. I leave you to the first flowers, and the tender stars of May.

One evening from the television room to which Carol had wandered in her nightgown with an orange on a plate, I began to hear a voice in a documentary: " . . . all medical science can to conquer it. The most fruitful source of study, and the best variation of the disease in which to try out certain new remedies, is that form in which it cruises in the bloodstreams of children under the name . . . " My mind spun helplessly like a wheel in a rut. Sick with horror, I strolled in and stood over her, bending down to help myself to an orange slice from the plate in her lap as on the TV screen a boy was put through familiar clinical tests for the instruction of the public. I should not have been surprised to see Dr. Scoville amble in. Were all my efforts to keep the truth from her, never to mention the name, the ceaseless censorship of word and tone, the hoarding of our secret from friends and neighbors, to collapse under this brutal mischance? "Lots of kids are worse off than you," I observed, striking a negligent pose against the wall. I patted my coat pockets. "Keep that, I want to get my pipe."

I shot on tiptoe to the kitchen, where I called Omar Howard. "Call Carol back. I'll explain later. Don't tell her I did this, but *call her back instantly and keep her on the telephone as long as you can.*"

"I understand, Mr. Wanderhope," said the young scholar, who was probably watching the same program. I think Omar knew.

Keeping the pre-teen-ager on the phone for an hour

was no trick at all in view of the recent birthday presents she had to report. She had gotten a new bicycle, half a dozen dresses, three pairs of shoes, two new leotards for ballet school, a crate of storybooks, assorted jewelry, a kitten, what would probably be her last doll, since she was now twelve, and a tape recorder costing two hundred dollars. It had been Mrs. Brodhag who had reined the madman in. "For God's sake, Mr. Wanderhope, she'll surely get suspicious. Now don't buy her any more. In fact, take the tape recorder back, or say it's for yourself, which it is anyway. And while I'm at it, don't be so obvious about getting her piano pieces on it."

I was sitting in the television room when Carol returned, carrying the kitten. She hadn't much to say, or did I fancy that? There was a variety show on now anyway, on which a guest comedian was going strong.

Straight man: "Lew, your comedy is too primitive. Times have changed. People don't want that belly laugh and pratfall stuff any more, they want adult, *intellectual* amusement. The inward chuckle, the smile of appreciation."

Comedian: "Rolling 'em in the aisles is good enough for me."

"You missed a good program," I said.

She looked down at her plate, to which she had returned an uneaten segment of orange. "My gums sting again," she said.

"Well, fine! That's what we want. Just enough soreness to show the medicine is taking effect, like last time."

"I think I'll go to bed. Come on, kitty."

The nobility, the reticence and dignity of that royal child cannot always be reported of the father. Dead-drunk and cold-sober, he wandered out to the garden in the cool of the evening, awaiting the coming of the Lord. No such advent taking place, he shook his fist at the sky and cried, "If you won't save her from pain, at least let me keep her from fear!" A brown thrush began his evening note, the ever favored, unendurable woodsong. I snatched up a rock from the ground and stoned it from the tree.

Afraid of leaving her to brood both on what she may have heard and on my absence, I went back into the house and to her bedroom. Each entrance there held its fear that a languid child would be found stretched out upon the bedclothes. I was glad to see her sitting up against the pillow, reading a book and stroking the puss for whom no name had as yet been found.

"Who's going to have a cup of cocoa with a man?"

She raised her eyes from the book. She put it aside. "O.K.," she said, getting up and into her pink robe.

Fixing the hot chocolate in the kitchen, I was happy to hear the piano begin in the parlor. It was a Chopin *Nocturne*, high among the pieces she had polished to perfection. Anxious to get it on tape, I stooped as unobtrusively as I could, after setting her cocoa on the piano, to switch on the nearby recorder. She glanced down at it and went on playing. I nodded to the cocoa steaming on a stack of sheet music, before wandering off to a chair.

After three months she reported headaches and trouble with her eyes. Here was noted also an increase in Dr. Scoville's charm. The slight complication was meningeal. "The disease can be kept at bay in the system while proliferating in the meninges, where for some reason the drug doesn't penetrate," he explained. "Why, we'll just leave her here in the hospital and take a spinal tap and see." The specimen extracted showed the ailment to be swirling richly in that sanctuary, into which massive doses of the Methotrexate had now to be injected directly.

So we were back in the Children's Pavilion, and there was again the familiar scene: the mothers with their nearly dead, the false face of mercy, the Slaughter of the Innocents. A girl with one leg came unsteadily down the hall between crutches, skillfully encouraged by nurses. Through the pane in a closed door a boy could be seen sitting up in bed, bleeding from everything in his head; a priest lounged alertly against the wall, ready to move in closer. In the next room a boy of five was having Methotrexate pumped into his skull, or, more accurately, was watching a group of mechanics gathered solemnly around the stalled machine. In the next a baby was sitting up watching a television set on which a panel show was in progress. Three experts were discussing the state of the contemporary theater. I paused in the doorway to listen. "I think writers like Tennessee Williams exaggerate the ugly side of life, the seamy side, it seems to me," observed a well-dressed female participant. "I fail to see what purpose is gained by that." A mother keeping watch at the next crib rose from her chair and turned the dial. There was a squawk of protest from the baby, who was evidently fascinated by the speaker's hat or the tone of her voice, or something else about the program, and the woman quickly tuned it back, making a comic face at me.

Among the parents and children, flung together in a hell of prolonged farewell, wandered forever the ministering vampires from Laboratory, sucking samples from bones and veins to see how went with each the enemy that had marked them all. And the doctors in their butchers' coats, who severed the limbs and gouged the brains and knifed the vitals where the demon variously dwelt, what did they think of these best fruits of ten million hours of dedicated toil? They hounded the culprit from organ to organ and joint to joint till nothing remained over which to practice their art: the art of prolonging sickness. Yet medicine had its own old aphorism: "Life is a fatal disease."

I rejoined in time the endless promenade of visitors pushing their treasures in wheel chairs. Among these was a beatnik adolescent trundling his younger sister. They were both very gay; one knew from their manner that she was going home soon. The youth was dressed in jeans and a black sweater. The beard was no doubt intended to be Bohemian but recalled, instead, the traditional figure of the hayseed. The pleasant spirit given off by their companionship made us join them, wheeling along side by side, up and down, back and forth, until some countertraffic forced us to break ranks. In one of these oncoming chairs was black-eyed Rachel Stein, propelled by her mother. The two girls instantly renewed the friendship begun the first time in, and it was obvious that they preferred now to be left together in the recreation room, where in any case a birthday party for another patient was in full swing. Mrs. Stein excused herself to dart after a disappearing doctor, and I looked around for Stein. As I neared the main lounge I heard voices raised in argument.

"These people who want to tell God how to run the universe," a man with a brick-red neck was saying, "they remind me of those people with five shares in some corporation who take up the entire stockholders' meeting telling the directors how to run their business."

I might have guessed who the object of the dressing down would be. Stein stood cornered behind the telephone booth, a carton of coffee in one hand and a smile on his face, obviously enjoying himself enormously. This was what he liked, proof of idiocy among the Positive Thinkers.

"I suppose you're going to tell me next I never met a payroll," he said, throwing me only the faintest sign of greeting so as not to interrupt the debate. Several visitors, mostly parents in various stages of vigil and dishevelment, listened or chimed in.

"You ought to be ashamed," a woman in an Easter bonnet told Stein. "Your race gave us our religion. It's a good thing the ancient prophets weren't like you or we wouldn't have any." Stein drank from his carton and waited; she had not yet delivered herself into his hands. "From ancient polytheism, the belief in lots of gods," the woman continued a little more eruditely, "the Hebrew nation led us on to the idea that there is only one."

"Which is just a step from the truth," said Stein, and dropped his carton into a wastebasket.

The woman began to show anger, squirming a bit on her leather chair. "We with our finite . . . "

"What baffles me is the comfort people find in the

idea that somebody dealt this mess. Blind and meaningless chance seems to me so much more congenial — or at least less horrible. Prove to me that there is a God and I will really begin to despair."

"It comes down to submitting to a wisdom greater than ours," said the man who had been attempting to focus the problem in terms of a stockholders' meeting. "A plan of which we can no more grasp the whole than a leaf can the forest of which it is a rustling part, or a grain of sand the seashore. What do you think when you look up at the stars at night?"

"I don't. I have enough to occupy me here."

"The Lord giveth and the Lord taketh away. What do you think of that?"

"I think it's a hell of a way to run a railroad."

"You ought to be ashamed!" the woman repeated with a further rise in spirit, not noticing a four-year-old patient watching the argument from a tricycle in the doorway. "Have you ever read your Bible?"

I nearly laughed. Where did she think he had got his pessimism? On what had he nurtured his despair if not on "Vanity of vanities," "All flesh is grass," "My tears have been my meat day and night," and "Is there no balm in Gilead; is there no physician there?"

Stein left his persecutors to join me in the hall, sending little Johnny Heard off on his tricycle with a pat on the head. We stood a moment comparing notes. Rachel was in for the very same thing as Carol, after all these months of solid remission on Methotrexate and the 6-MP still to go. We sought out the girls in the recreation room, where they were getting on beautifully together. They didn't want any part of us. "How about a drink?" Stein proposed.

In my present need Stein might seem the last company I ought to seek. Yet in another sense he was precisely what I wanted at my side, the Devil's advocate off whom to bounce my speculations, the rock against which to hurl my yearnings and my thoughts, to test and prove them truly, an office that mealy-mouthed piety could not have performed. He was the goalkeeper past whom I must get my puck.

"There is so much we don't know," I said as, walking down the street, we resumed the debate where we had left off last time. "Newton knew it, who told us so much we do know. We play like children on the shore — out there is the measureless sea. How do you explain — well, a thing like what happened on the road to Damascus?"

"Do I have to explain every case of hysterical blindness? How do we know it happened, anyway? It's related only in the Acts, which Luke wrote. Paul himself never mentions it, and him a man who talked about himself at the drop of a hat."

"He said Christ was revealed to him, as to a child born untimely. That may be what he's referring to. I think it's in Corinthians. And there's the incident of the viper and the fire."

"I'm told Orientals walk barefoot across hot coals with no ill effects."

"So such things happen." Something made me look up. I saw, her arms spread along the parapet of the second-story roof from which the mice were visible, the woman with the Easter bonnet, gazing up into the dirty spring evening. "Do you believe any of the miracles attributed to Christ?" I said quickly, perhaps because I had looked just in time to see her brush her eye, under the cheap pink veil.

Stein gave his snort, this time somewhat more finely shaded than usual. He jerked his head back toward the hospital. "Who do you expect to see take up his bed and walk in there?"

As we strolled along, for all the world like friends out taking the evening air rather than two men wringing each other's hearts like empty dishrags, we encountered a phenomenon that under the circumstances could hardly be ignored. A street-corner evangelist was hurling plangent metaphors rapidly into space.

"Would you like to call Heaven tonight? You can reverse the charges, you know. Oh, yes, brother, reverse the charges." He swung from his audience, a girl with a jump rope and a Chinese laundryman pausing in the gutter with his pushcart to eat a candy bar, toward us as we approached. "Oh, yes, brother, reverse the charges. *He'll* accept them. He's paid for your call with the ultimate price — His Son Jesus Christ! It's all paid for, all on the house, all for free! Just pick up the phone and tell the operator — that's the Holy Ghost, you know — 'Get me Heaven, please. Put me through to God Almighty!'"

We shuffled on in silence. Stein had the grace not to smile at the ally I had picked up along the way. I observed after a moment:

"Someone has pointed out that nothing proves the validity of the Church so much as its ability to survive its own representatives. It's got to be divine to stand up against them."

"I have never been convinced by that argument — it's from one of the witty Catholics, isn't it? You might as well say it about the Ku Klux Klan."

"That's no analogy. In that case the members are no worse than the principles. In this, the principle is always supremely there for us to match up to or fall short of."

Stein shrugged and gave a grunt. I felt I had gotten past the goalkeeper and scored a point. We were passing a pushcart vendor selling sprigs of dogwood. I had brought plenty of that from the country this morning. I asked Stein, after another silence, whether he had ever heard the legend that the Cross had been made of dogwood and that supposedly explained the cross shaped vaguely into the grain of its heartwood, like that on the back of the Sardinian donkey for its having borne Our Lord into Jerusalem on his triumphal day. Stein said that he had never heard of that. I myself would never chop down a dogwood in order to check on the legend, or imagine that it would survive close scrutiny. But for the yearning spirit there is in any case another, that Christ miraculously guaranteed to the flowering tree that it would never again grow to a size great enough to hew a cross from.

In the bar, I chided Stein for what he had said to the woman in the Easter hat, on the ground that Westminster Hospital was no place to pull rugs out from under mothers. He agreed, with the assurance that he never did that to mothers, or even to men unless they could take it, but informed me that the woman in this case was not the mother but an aunt — the mother was on another floor in the same hospital, having a malignancy edited from her foot. This brought Stein perilously close to his role of clown, and I could feel my shoulders threaten to shake in preparation for the only response possible to this eager trowel work with the Absurd. It didn't take much.

"Was the man who talked about stockholders' meetings the father?"

"No," said Stein, as though he had been waiting for me to ask that question, "the father is in a mental institution."

Stein watched me until my sobs of laughter had subsided, smiling uneasily as I gasped, "Have you no heart, man?" and brushing cigarette ashes from his horrible green sleeve.

Wiping my eyes, I asked whether he didn't think even aunts deserved to have their belief that those who mourned would be comforted, safeguarded from the scourge of intellect. Here I sensed a quiver of indignation as he launched a review of the Beatitudes aimed at finding one — "just one" — that held water when examined squarely in the light of reality. The poor in spirit would have to imagine for themselves any kingdom of heaven, as the pure in heart would any God for themselves; the merciful obtained no more mercy than the cruel; the meek would have to inherit anything they ever got; and so on. There was, however, one Beatitude with which one need not quarrel — could I guess which it was? It was not one of the official nine, having been delivered separately on the road to Calvary. I gave up. " 'Blessed are the wombs that never bare, and the paps that never gave suck,' " Stein said. "Could this be the Son of Man preparing himself for those final words against the black sky, the last, cosmic turn of the wheel of agony, the hoax at last seen through: 'My God, my God, why hast thou forsaken me?' "

"You mean you're not *sure?* Why, man, that's great! For the rest of us, who like to hug that little doubt we so desperately need today — what faith was to folk of another time — the ray of hope. Oh, how grateful we are for that uncertainty! Our salvation almost. Go thy way, thy doubt hath made thee whole. Bartender, two more!"

My spirits began to rise — genuinely, not in another spasm of unstable mirth. From nowhere, I had suddenly that conviction that we would beat the rap, that Carol and Rachel would be among those who were around when the Drug came. *Some* would; why not they? My mood continued to ascend. The wall-motto moralists quite rightly call bottom the place from which there is nowhere to go but up, the floor against which the swimmer kicks himself lightly toward the surface once again.

As we left the tavern, I remarked, "Well, we could go on arguing for hours, I suppose. As man has in fact for centuries about these things. There's as much to be said for one side as for the other. Fifty-fifty."

"Not quite. One charge can be brought against your point of view that can't against mine: wishful thinking. Believers believe what they want to believe. I would like to believe it, too, but deny that an honest man can. Unbelief is to that extent less suspect than faith."

We trudged along a moment longer, during which I debated with myself whether to say what I was thinking. I spoke up.

"One doubts that you don't enjoy thinking or saying what you do, at least a little, Stein. The side of man that loves to hate, to rub in the horrible, even revel in it.

Psychiatrists have even got a name for it, I think. Algolagnia, or something like that."

We passed in due course the church of St. Catherine, from which a pair of people were contentedly emerging after their evening devotionals. Here a vibration of anger escaped Stein that was not put into words, but that I felt had given me a flash of illumination into his spirit — something that might even be held to confirm the theory of my friend to which I had been needled into giving audible expression. Stein resented the sedative power of religion, or rather the repose available to those blissfully ignorant that the medicament was a fictitious blank. In this exile from peace of mind to which his reason doomed him, he was like an insomniac driven to awaken sleepers from dreams illegitimately won by going around shouting, "Don't you realize it was a placebo!" Thus it seemed to me that what you were up against in Stein was not logic rampant, but frustrated faith. He could not forgive God for not existing.

When we returned to the Pavilion of Children, Mrs. Stein greeted us in the corridor. "You should see the two of them playing together," she said. "Come look."

We stood in the recreation room doorway. In a pandemonium of television noise, piano music being thumped out by a volunteer as youngsters banged drums and shook tambourines to its rhythm, Rachel and Carol sat side by side at a table, twisting into being paper flowers for children less fortunate. Mrs. Stein had quoted us that bit as we came down the hall with a surprising minimum of rue. "Aren't they just too sweet together?" she beamed in the doorway.

"Lifelong friends," said Stein, who gave, and asked, no quarter.

My conversations with Stein are almost all I am re-calling of my relations with other parents because they were vital to my concerns, not because they — and the brief skirmish I overheard in the lounge — were typical of human intercourse there. Far from it. Airing the ab-solutes is no longer permitted in polite society, save where a Stein and a Wanderhope meet and knock their heads together, but I do not think this is due to apathy or frivolity, or because such pursuits are vain, though one pant for God as the hart after water-brooks. There is another reason why we chatter of this and that while our hearts burn within us.

We live this life by a kind of conspiracy of grace: the common assumption, or pretense, that human existence is "good" or "matters" or has "meaning," a glaze of charm or humor by which we conceal from one another and perhaps even ourselves the suspicion that it does not, and our conviction in times of trouble that it is over-priced — something to be endured rather than enjoyed. Nowhere does this function more than in precisely such a slice of hell as a Children's Pavilion, where the basic truths would seem to mock any state of mind other than rage and despair. Rage and despair are indeed carried about in the heart, but privately, to be let out on special occasions, like savage dogs for exercise, occasions in soli-tude when God is cursed, birds stoned from the trees or the pillow hammered in darkness. In the ward lounge itself, a scene in which a changing collection of char-

2 1 5

acters are waiting for a new medicine that might as well be called Godot, the conversation is indistinguishable from that going on at the moment in the street, a coffee break at the office from which one is absent, or a dinner party to which one could not accept an invitation. Even the exchange of news about their children has often the quality of gossip. An earful of it would be incredible to an uninvolved spectator, not to its principals. Quiet is requested for the benefit of the other parents. One holds his peace in obedience to a tacit law as binding as if it were framed on a corridor wall with a police officer on hand to see that it was enforced: "No fuss." This is all perhaps nothing more than the principle of sportsmanship at its highest, given in return for the next man's. Even Stein had it in no small degree, for all his seeming refusal to wish me good hunting in my spiritual quest. Perhaps he was trying to tell me in as nice a way as he could that there was no game in those woods. His grim little jokes on the barricades were in their way part of this call to courage.

But while human abilities to sustain this sportsmanship vary, none is unlimited. Twice I had the uneasy experience of witnessing a crackup in the ranks of those one comes to think of, not too farfetchedly, as one's outfit — that moment when the thin membrane to which our sanity is entrusted splits and breaks asunder, spilling violence in every direction.

There was a mother Carol and I saw in every hospitalization, taking care of a four-year-old boy who was by now a scarecrow. She lived in Ohio, and her husband came only on weekends, or when he could get off from work. Her name was May Schwartz, and her comely Jewish bulk, her ripe yolky warmth and vitality typified a certain order of female appeal, often irresistible to the Gentile eye. Though she was neither very young nor notably shapely any more, one always marked her passage down the corridor. Wearing high heels to offset her short height, rather than the "sensible" shoes that would certainly have eased her thousand marches to and from her vegetable, she would bounce along with a towel and wash basin or a glass of soda pop in her hands, and return any nod of greeting, as you passed her wheeling your own charge, by smiling and rolling her eyes up to the ceiling as if to say, "Gawd." I heard her say it aloud when told in the lounge that a rabbi had arrived to call on Sammy, rolling her eyes again as she rose to receive him. I happened to see the rabbi go into Sammy's room, where he put on a black skullcap and stood at the foot of the bed murmuring something, before thrusting the cap back into his overcoat pocket and hurrying away again, looking a little foolish. Mrs. Schwartz said that her husband arranged for these pastoral visits, in which she "saw no harm."

One night I was sleeping on the leather couch in the lounge, or trying to. I was too excited by the news, just acquired, that I might take Carol home tomorrow. I was staying overnight so that we could make an early start in the morning. Carol herself had been full of beans all evening, and I was still laughing over a story she had told me about Stein, one Rachel had related in confidence and over which I had been sworn to secrecy. One Sunday morning when Stein had been sleeping late, Rachel, then four, feeling sorry for her bald daddy, had decided to do something about it. From locks of hair snipped from old dolls and sewn together on a piece of oilcloth, she made a wig, or toupee, the underside of which she then generously slathered with glue and, stealing into the bedroom, affixed to her father's pate. This naturally awakened Stein from sleep, and more particularly, according to accounts by which he tried later to explain his resulting behavior, from a bad dream he had been having. Perhaps the dream had been inspired by the intrusive sensation itself, in that split second of time in which we are told these things can occur. At any rate, he had kicked his legs out of bed and run wildly into the bathroom, there to be confronted by his image in the glass, newly patched with thatch of varying hues and textures. The picture of Stein blinking confusedly at himself, perhaps befuddled by some impression remaining from his dream that he had indeed sprouted fresh feathers, and then the sequel as he removed what he saw, had me in stitches. Delayed fatigue, together with the sudden release from the last round of anxiety, left me an easy prey to hysteria, and I lay there in the dark shaking with laughter. The fit of mirth prolonged itself uncontrollably, and I finally had to smother my convulsions in a handkerchief. There was a stir behind the thin wall separating the lounge from the next room, where Mrs. Schwartz spent her nights on a cot. Then I heard the door of that room open. The faint scuff of slippered feet followed, and Mrs. Schwartz herself stood in the open doorway of the lounge.

She had on a flannel robe, under which could be seen the legs of a pair of pajamas. Her face was invisible since the lounge was dark, but against the faint glow cast by a corridor light I could see her arms go up and knew that she had her own hands to her face. From her motionless figure now issued a series of broken, muffled sounds very similar — I now sensed, as a chill went up my spine — to those that had a moment ago greeted her own ears. She had mistaken the nature of my hysterics and been moved to offer their echo in a passionate outburst of her own. She was, in any case, not the solid rock for which we had been accustomed to take her.

As she came forward into the room I rose. She whispered for me not to do so, urging me back down onto the couch with a force that dropped me abruptly once more on the leather cushion. She sank to her knees and began suddenly to beat the arm of the couch with both fists, at the same time babbling incoherently. The words came out in a stream, English, Yiddish, oaths and imprecations, blasphemies and entreaties I could not hope to reproduce. "All they can do is kill mice!" she said in a kind of whispered scream. I grasped her shoulders, and, when this did no good, her wrists. Whereupon she wrenched her arms free and threw them around my neck, in a spasm of emotion that might have been mistaken, by someone glancing into the darkened room, for an amorous clutch. Which in a mad sort of way it probably was. For as suddenly as she had begun she stopped, went to a chair, blew her nose, and said, "It's a funny thing about two people going through something like this. There are things husband and wife just can't tell each other that they can a third person."

"Tell" each other! I thought, what in God's name has she told me? As if sensing this, she immediately added, "I guess I mean do to each other. You have no wife, but I've got news for you. You think you could have shared this?" She shook her head, and though the illumination from the corridor was too dim for me to make out her face, I could imagine her shrugged mouth and closed eyes. "Two people can't share unhappiness. You think probably if you had her, 'Well, we could go through this together. It would bring us closer together. Leaning on each other.' " Again the headshake, with news for me. "They lean away from each other. Two people can't share grief. In fact — " She broke off, as though momentarily debating the prudence of the revelation on the tip of her tongue, then making it anyway. "In some ways it drives them apart, an explosion between them. No, that's not it either." She lowered her head, and for a moment I feared a revival of hysterics. She went on, as though the paradox of what she was elucidating was an aid to objectivity, "When this first came to us, was fresh, the wound, there were times when I resented my husband. Because he, what's the word I want?" She snapped her fingers. "Presumed. Presumed to share what was basically a woman's grief. Horning in on a sorrow the woman is sole proprietor of. Isn't that ridiculous? But there it is, a chapter in what's this man's name who writes about the war between the sexes. Can you beat it?" she softly cried, bringing her fist down ominously now on the arm of the chair, but only once, and that like a public speaker, or actor, well in control of his effects. I sat mesmerized in my own seat, transfixed in perhaps the most amazing midnight I had ever lived through, yet one possessing, in the dreamy dislocations of which it formed a part, a weird, bland naturalness like that of a Chirico landscape, full of shadows infinitely longer than the objects casting them. "And no doubt Schwartz has some of the same resentment as mine. Never is this stated between two people, but it's there. Driving this — wedge between them, so that a woman can't break down to her husband but she can very well fling herself for a moment on another man's breast, while Schwartz at this very minute is probably with that . . . Well, never mind. Does this make sense to you?"

"Why, I think I can see where . . ."

"Well then make room in your head for the exact opposite explanation. That we keep outbursts from one another because we owe it to the other person. Out of a *feeling* for the other party. We owe it to them not to wish on them what they keep from us in their own moments. All this you're learning about marriage," she went on, like a chiropractor manipulating his subject's head in a series of violent, though supposedly salubrious, contrasts. "So your wife," she went on in a manner suggesting that she absorbed as much gossip as she dispensed in these watches of the night, "would never have come to you in the way I just did. To somebody else maybe, yes, but to you, no." She brushed at her cheeks and rose. "So now how about a cigarette?" She turned to switch on the light, glancing then at the electric coffee urn always standing on a table there, to see if it was connected. "Let's plug this thing in and heat up what's in it."

As we smoked a cigarette and drank our coffee, she told me something about her husband's work. He was publicity director for an Akron shoe factory, much prized by the firm though beset by envious rivals waiting to ambush him. She hoped we would get a chance to meet when next he came to the hospital. We would probably have a lot to say to each other.

The second drama was of a different sort and by no means as instructive, except on a more elementary level.

Off the main corridor was a room in which the doctors held daily consultations among themselves on all the cases then on the floor, and into which individual ones sometimes drew parents for a word in private. One day as I walked past its closed door, I heard behind it a shrill man's voice upbraiding somebody. "Then why didn't you switch to the other drug sooner, you ── " The epithet, if such it was, was drowned out by the scraping of a chair. This became immediately an unmistakable scuffle, in which shouts and overturned chairs mingled in equal measure. I froze, wondering whether to rush in. I had heard that crazed parents on rare occasions physically attacked their children's doctors, and indeed had once noticed an armed guard unobtrusively but watchfully haunting the ward. I could understand this behavior as an exaggeration of a normal reaction, perhaps even a normal irrationality, from a disquieting sensation that had suddenly gone through me the evening Dr. Cameron had come to the house with his news. *I had hated him physically*. I had wanted to bash his teeth in. The vituperation continued, varied only by counterprotestations and pleas to "control yourself" in a voice now recognizable as that of Dr. Scoville. When an especially alarming thud was heard, I opened the door and ran in.

Dr. Scoville, in his white coat, was standing behind a desk, which he had evidently been circling to keep between himself and his client ── a man I recognized as an out-of-town father whom I had seen wheeling a child in a perambulator. He had red hair and bulging blue eyes that gave him a look of subdued frenzy the best of times. Now his face resembled a pot of tomatoes about to boil over. There was an X ray on an illuminated panel, whose portents the doctor had probably been trying to interpret when the man had gone out of control. In a blaze of deprecation now broadened to include the hospital, to which he should never have removed his child from the one in New Jersey, he shouted, " — progress! I understand you can now induce malignancies in normal tissues!" I stepped in at this point and tried to calm him. This made him turn on me, perhaps in a kind of escape: he may have sensed by now that he was making a spectacle of himself, as we sometimes do in outbursts, and welcomed an adversary against whose intrusions he had a more legitimate complaint. I was frankly scared, and noticed with relief that two male residents were trotting through the open doorway, attracted by the commotion. They succeeded between them in quieting the man down, and I left all four of them trying to settle down again to a more sober discussion of matters.

I saw Dr. Scoville later in the day and, itching with curiosity of course, mentioned the incident. But he refused to discuss it beyond a word of thanks to me for stepping in. "I quite understand those things," he said, and, opening a metal chart folder, turned to my problems.

I offer these two vignettes of human collapse, not for their own sakes, or even as necessarily vital links in the narrative, but as preliminaries to describing the moment — not a very pretty story itself — when I reached the end of my own tether.

fifteen

ONE TIME in that criminal winter, when the lights of Christmas sprouted in a thousand windows and the mercies of Methotrexate were drawing to a close, we went in for our fifth hospitalization. Now we were to have our horizons widened. Anterior bleeding is not so bad, but posterior calls for cauterization, as well as packing, back into the throat. "Oh, Daddy, I can't stand it," said my spattered burden as I carried her from the treatment room back to bed. It is one of the few cries of protest I ever heard from the thoroughbred, of whom I bear true and faithful witness. The stigmata were fresh: the wound in the breast from a new aspiration, the prints in the hands from the intravenous and transfusion needles to which the arms were once again spread as she watched television with a reassembled smile. On the screen were unfolding again a few reels of the dear old clowns. The comic for whom rolling 'em in the aisles had been sufficient was doing the narrating, only this time on the side of the intellectuals.

"You see, Daddy? How they wait for the pie, then take

their time wiping it off and all? A ritual. He calls it that too."

Stein and his Rachel were not here this time, but the Great Debate went forward between two voices now scarcely for a moment silent in my brain.

"I ask, my Lord, permission to despair."

"On what grounds?"

"The fairy is now a troll. The spine is gone. She supports herself on her breastbone."

"Do you do as well?"

"Do you exist?"

"If I say yes, it will only be as a voice in your mind. Make me say it then, and be quiet."

"Are God and Herod then one?"

"What do you mean?"

"The Slaughter of the Innocents. Who creates a perfect blossom to crush it? Children dying in this building, mice in the next. It's all the same to Him who marks the sparrow's fall."

"I forgive you."

"I cannot say the same."

I awoke from a doze in the bedside chair that night remembering, for some reason, the occasion a few weeks before when I had taken Carol to the Blood Bank at the school she attended.

Wanderhope was being siphoned by the Red Cross, and she was watching, peeking through the curtain screening off the double line of donors. "Opium den," she said, exaggerating the words so as not to have to speak above a whisper. The conceit amused me no end. I finished out my gift in fantasies of myself and Mrs. Baldridge in the next bed, and the minister's wife next to her, lying in an opium trance, haggard devotees of the fix, lost in debaucheries beyond belief.

Seeing she was asleep, both arms spread to the trailers from the bottles overhead, I stole out to the lounge for a smoke. I had hopes of a drink from the flask I now carried regularly on my person, but I found a three-hundred-pound woman pacing there in a rumpled housedress, a cigarette with a sagging inch of ash hanging from her mouth.

"Boy, dis place," she said. "When me and my little girl come in here, she di'n't have nuttin' but leukemia. Now she's got ammonia." I listened, unbelieving. "Ammonia. Dat's serious. She's in a oxygen tent, and I can't smoke there. It's a tough break for her because, like I say, at first she di'n't have nuttin' but a touch of leukemia. I don't believe I ever heard of dat before. What is it?"

". . . Now have I permission to despair, my Lord?"

"How do you mean?"

"That woman. How ludicrous can grief become?"

"What else?"

"That birthday party in the playroom this afternoon for Johnny Heard. *Leukemic children with funny hats.* How slapstick can tragedy get? Is nobody seeing to the world? Is it run on no principles whatever? The children and next door the rats . . . "

"They are one to the Good Lord, who loves them all."

Here a burst of mocking laughter suffices to express its alternative: the Voiceless Void, the bland stupor of eternity.

The Meticorten did only a third as well this time around, but home we went with the marrow only thirty per cent of normal, and a pocketful of a new drug. Glad we were to get out too, because an epidemic of staphylo-coccus was raging through the ward and half the inno-cents lay in oxygen tents. Two or three of the more for-tunate had died, and the fat woman's girl, too, was re-leased from harm by her pneumonia — the old man's friend, as we used to call it.

We had other blessings to be thankful for. Carol's gold hair began to come out by the handful, proof that the new drug was taking hold, for hair loss was one of its side effects. She was soon balder than her father. I tried to get her outside by suggesting she wear a scarf, without avail. Finally I got her into New York, where she was fitted for a wig — a transformation so perfect that she now willingly bound her head in a kerchief. Pending the next marrow test, we looked for other incidental signs that the drug was taking effect. One was a depressed white count. Carol's went down steadily, though not without its hazards since that left the patient wide open to infection — a delicate point of orchestration. One night I found her lying on the bed on her side, hugging a globe of the world for the pleasure of feeling its cool metal against her skin. I poked a thermometer into her mouth and found she had a temperature of a hundred and two. Dr. Cameron came and dosed her with his broad-spectrum antibiotics, but suggested she go into the hospital anyway for safety's sake.

I walked out past St. Catherine's to the bar and grill and back again so often through so many hospitaliza-tions that I cannot remember which time it was that I stopped in the church on the way back to sit down and rest. I was dead-drunk and stone-sober and bone-tired, my head split and numbed by the plague of voices in eternal disputation. I knew why I was delaying my return to the hospital. The report on the morning's aspiration would be phoned up to the ward from the laboratory any minute, and what I died to learn I dreaded to hear.

I got up and walked to the center aisle, where I stood looking out to the high altar and the soaring windows. I turned around and went to the rear corner, where stood the little shrine to St. Jude, Patron of Lost Causes and Hopeless Cases. Half the candles were burning. I took a taper and lit another. I was alone in the church. The gentle flames wavered and shattered in a mist of tears spilling from my eyes as I sank to the floor.

"I do not ask that she be spared to me, but that her life be spared to her. Or give us a year. We will spend it as we have the last, missing nothing. We will mark the dance of every hour between the snowdrop and the snow: crocus to tulip to violet to iris to rose. We will note not only the azalea's crimson flowers but the red halo that encircles a while the azalea's root when her petals are shed, also the white halo that rings for a week the foot of the old catalpa tree. Later we will prize the chrysanthemums which last so long, almost as long as paper flowers, perhaps because they know in blooming not to bloom. We will seek out the leaves turning in the little-praised bushes and the unadvertised trees. Everyone loves the sweet, neat blossom of the hawthorn in spring, but who lingers over the olive drab of her leaf in autumn? We will. We will note the lost yellows in the tangles of that bush that spills over the Howards' stone wall, the meek hues among which it seems to hesitate before committing itself to red, and next year learn its name. We will seek out these modest subtleties so lost in the blare of oaks and maples, like flutes and woodwinds drowned in brasses and drums. When winter comes, we will let no snow fall ignored. We will again watch the first blizzard from her window like figures locked snug in a glass paperweight. 'Pick one out and follow it to the ground!' she will say again. We will feed the plain birds that stay to cheer us through the winter, and when spring returns we shall be the first out, to catch the snowdrop's first white whisper in the wood. All this we ask, with the remission of our sins, in Christ's name. Amen."

Mrs. Morganthaler was trundling the supper trays to the recreation room when I got back to the ward, for those who could eat there. Carol was asleep in bed. Her arms were spread to the perennial vessels, one white, one red, hanging above the bed. The special nurse rose from her corner chair and whispered that now might be a good time for her to slip out for a bite of supper. I nodded, and she left, carrying her magazine under her arm.

I stood a while over the quietly breathing child. She had her wig off, and now without her hair I could see how perfectly shaped her head was. Child of the pure, unclouded brow . . . The stigmata were more marked than ever, those in the hands dark and numerous from many needles, the wound in the breast fresh under its cotton pad. The short strip of adhesive tape over the cotton bore its usual gold star, given for good behavior and valor under fire.

As I stood there, I sensed the door being quietly opened. Turning, I saw the face of Dr. Romulo, the young Filipino resident, thrust shyly into the room. He beckoned me out into the corridor. He took my arm and led me off a few steps. His face had the solemn expression of one bearing important news.

"We just got the marrow report back," he said. "It's down to six per cent. Practically normal. Carol's in remission."

sixteen

"THE TROUBLE with doubling recipes," said Mrs. Brodhag, "is that some ingredients do a little more than double when you put in twice as much of them. Matter of proportion. Like the fellow says about people being created equal, well, some are more equal than others."

I laughed extendedly at this, watching her complete her handiwork. From the pastry bag she squeezed eight green rosettes around the rim of the cake with meticulous care, then cleaned out the bag thoroughly for the eight red rosettes which were to alternate with them. The field of the frosting was white. Once again she washed out the bag to write, with a blue icing also separately mixed, Carol's name in her flawless Palmer Method. She had been up since dawn.

"See that she gets plenty but the other kids do too," Mrs. Brodhag said as she set the creation in my two hands. "It's not the kind of thing I like to see ice cream glopped on top of, but if that's what they want to do I guess we can't object. And tell her there'll be another ready for her when she comes home, though I don't imagine she has to be told that. Don't lay things on too thick, like I keep telling you."

After parking the car in New York, I picked the boxed cake up carefully from the seat and, pushing the door shut with my knee, carried it down the street. A short distance up ahead I could see Mrs. Morano, the night nurse, turn into the church of St. Catherine for her morning prayers. I shifted the package to one hand in order to open the door. I walked to the front of the church, which had its normal smattering of worshipers. I set the cake down on an empty pew and joined the kneeling figures.

When I rose, Mrs. Morano was standing at the edge of the chancel. We whispered together a moment in greeting as we moved up the aisle.

"You heard about Carol," I said.

"Yes, it's exciting. That's why I'm so sorry about this."

"What?"

"The infection. It's been going through the ward like wildfire. Half of the kids are in oxygen tents."

"Carol?"

She nodded. "They had me phone you this morning, but you'd left. The new drug does depress the white count so terribly, of course, and leave them wide open to infection. It's the old story — you can pick anything up in a hospital."

"Staph?"

"I don't know. They took a blood culture, but it takes a while for the organisms to grow out. They're putting Chloromycetin into her, I think. Maybe you'd better go up."

I hurried into the hospital. One look at Carol and I

knew it was time to say good-by. The invading germ, or germs, had not only ravaged her bloodstream by now, but had broken out on her body surface in septicemic discolorations. Her foul enemy had his will of her well at last. One of the blotches covered where they were trying to insert a catheter, and spread down along a thigh. By afternoon it had traveled to the knee, and by the next, gangrened. Dr. Scoville could not have been kinder.

"Someone has ordered another tank of oxygen," he told me that afternoon in the corridor, "but I think you'll agree it won't be necessary. . . . Well, hello there, Randy, you're going home today." Up, up, my head, for the sake of that childhood whom there is none in heaven to love, and none to love on earth so much as you. Up, up! "I've left orders for all the morphine she needs. She'll slip away quietly. She doesn't know us now. It's just as well, because there isn't much in the new drug, if it's any consolation. We have a co-operative study on it, and the remissions are few and brief, and suspect because of the incidence of Meticorten administered with it. We can never be sure it wasn't the Meticorten in this case. It would only have meant another short reprieve — no pardon." He sighed and went his busy way, to the ends of the earth.

I went back into the room. The nurse was taking her blood pressure. "Almost none at all," she whispered. "It's just as well. Only a matter of hours now at the most." The wig was on a globe of the world on the table. The hands were free of needles now, spread out quietly on the counterpane, with their stigmata to which no more would be added. Her breathing slowed, each breath like a caught sob. But once she smiled a little, and, bending closer, I heard her call something to a comrade on another bicycle. They were flying home from school together, down the hill. "All her dreams are pleasant," the nurse murmured. I was thinking of a line of old poetry. "Death loves a shining mark." Now the flower-stem veins were broken, the flower-stalk of the spine destroyed. But through the troll I saw the fairy still, on her flying wheels, the sun in her hair and in the twinkling spokes. I had seen her practicing the piano in her leotard, there were so many things to do and so little time to do them in. I remembered how little labor the sprite had given her mother, so eager was she to be born, so impatient To Be.

The nurse stepped outside a moment, and I moved quickly from the foot of the bed around to the side, whispering rapidly in our moment alone:

"The Lord bless thee, and keep thee: The Lord make his face shine upon thee, and be gracious unto thee: The Lord lift up his countenance upon thee, and give thee peace."

Then I touched the stigmata one by one: the prints of the needles, the wound in the breast that had for so many months now scarcely ever closed. I caressed the perfectly shaped head. I bent to kiss the cheeks, the breasts that would now never be fulfilled, that no youth would ever touch. "Oh, my lamb."

The lips curled in another smile, one whose secret I thought I knew. I recognized it without the aid of the gaze, now sealed forever from mine, with which it had come to me so often throughout her childhood. It was the expression on her face when her homework was going well, the shine of pride at a column of figures mastered or a poem to spring successfully forged. It was the smile of satisfaction worn at the piano when a new composition had been memorized, on her bicycle when, gripping its vanquished horns, she had ridden past me on her first successful solo around the yard. Sometimes, as on that Saturday morning, she would turn the smile shyly toward me, taking added pleasure in my approval.

But this time the experience was not to be shared. She was going alone. Even without the eyes to help communicate it, there was a glow of the most intense concentration on her face, with that wariness of error or shortcoming that had always made it so complete and so characteristic. She had never seemed more alive than now, when she was gathering all the life within her for the proper discharge of whatever this last assignment might have been. Was it a sum of figures or a poem to nature she was undertaking in her dream? Or a difficult, delicate spray of notes, or the first ecstatic journey on the two-wheeler, with the promise of liberty on summer roads unfolding far ahead? I bent again to whisper a question in her ear, but there was no answer — only the most remote sense of flight upon the face. It shone like a star about to burst and, in bursting, yield me all its light at once — could I but bear the gift.

Even her wearied limbs had for the moment this tension, a vibrancy as of a drawn bow. But as the hours wore on, they seemed to slacken, and her features to relax as well. Perhaps the mission had been accomplished, and the hour of rest was at hand. Once, later that afternoon, the smile parted her lips again, this time widely enough to show that her gums were dripping. The enemy was pouring out of every crevice at last. The sight of these royal children pitted against this bestiality had always consumed me with a fury so blind I had had often to turn my face away. Now I was glad Carol could not see me standing there, alone, at last, on holy ground.

She went her way in the middle of the afternoon, borne from the dull watchers on a wave that broke and crashed beyond our sight. In that fathomless and timeless silence one does look rather wildly about for a clock, in a last attempt to fix the lost spirit in time. I had guessed what the hands would say. Three o'clock. The children were putting their schoolbooks away, and getting ready to go home.

After some legal formalities I went into the room once more to say good-by. I had once read a book in which the hero had complained, in a similar farewell taken of a woman, that it was like saying good-by to a statue. I wished it were so now. She looked finally like some mangled flower, or like a bird that had been pelted to earth in a storm. I knew that under the sheet she would look as though she had been clubbed to death. As for the dignity of man, this one drew forth a square of cloth, and, after honking like a goose, pocketed his tears.

The bartender had finished cleaning up after some last late lunchers and was polishing the glasses for the evening's trade. After I'd had six or seven drinks, he said to me, "No more. That must be the tenth muddler you've snapped in two." Perhaps he was hearing the voices too . . .

Passing the church of St. Catherine on the way to the car, I suddenly remembered the cake. I went inside, out of curiosity. It was still there on the pew, undisturbed. I picked it up and started out with it. An incoming wor-

236

shiper took frowning note of my unsteady career through the lobby door.

Outside, I paused on the sidewalk, one foot on the bottom step. I turned and looked up at the Figure still hanging as ever over the central doorway, its arms outspread among the sooted stones and strutting doves.

I took the cake out of the box and balanced it a moment on the palm of my hand. Disturbed by something in the motion, the birds started from their covert and flapped away across the street. Then my arm drew back and let fly with all the strength within me. Before the mind snaps, or the heart breaks, it gathers itself like a clock about to strike. It might even be said one pulls himself together to disintegrate. The scattered particles of self — love, wood thrush calling, homework sums, broken nerves, rag dolls, one Phi Beta Kappa key, gold stars, lamplight smiles, night cries, and the shambles of contemplation — are collected for a split moment like scraps of shrapnel before they explode.

It was miracle enough that the pastry should reach its target at all, at that height from the sidewalk. The more so that it should land squarely, just beneath the crown of thorns. Then through scalded eyes I seemed to see the hands free themselves of the nails and move slowly toward the soiled face. Very slowly, very deliberately, with infinite patience, the icing was wiped from the eyes and flung away. I could see it fall in clumps to the porch steps. Then the cheeks were wiped down with the same sense of grave and gentle ritual, with all the kind sobriety of one whose voice could be heard saying, "Suffer the little children to come unto me . . . for of such is the kingdom of heaven."

Then the scene dissolved itself in a mist in which my legs could no longer support their weight, and I sank down to the steps. I sat on its worn stones, to rest a moment before going on. Thus Wanderhope was found at that place which for the diabolists of his literary youth, and for those with more modest spiritual histories too, was said to be the only alternative to the muzzle of a pistol: the foot of the Cross.

seventeen

SUMMER PASSED into autumn, and when in No-
vember a few white flakes sifted down out of the sky,
Mrs. Brodhag decided to make the journey to her sister
in Seattle of which she had for so long restively spoken.
Perhaps she would make "other connections" there, in
view of my having the house on the market. If I sold it
— a result little foreshadowed by the processions march-
ing through it behind an ever-changing leadership of
brokers — and did move into a city apartment, I would
hardly be needing her help. The trip to the airport was
the first down the Parkway since the days when we had
made so many. " — In both our prayers — " she raged in
my ear against the roar of jets. I pressed into her hand a
St. Christopher medal, extricated with difficulty from the
chain of the crucifix with which it had become entangled
in my pocket. We smiled as she nodded thanks. Then
she was a bird in the sky, then a bee, then nothing.

It was as many months again before I could bring myself to explore at any length the bright front bedroom,
then only because the sudden sale of the house required

239

its cleaning out. Dresses and toys and bureau articles were put into boxes and carried into the garage for the charity truck to haul away. Among the books and papers in the large desk drawer was a class letter from the sixth grade, a monumental scroll on which each individual note was pasted, wound upon two sticks like an ancient document. I read a few before stowing it into a carton of things to be kept for a still further future. One was a note from a boy reputed to have lost his heart to her, commanding her early return and with a P.S. reading, "You and I up in a tree, K-I-S-S-I-N-G." Into the carton were also tucked the home movies still sealed in their original tins. At last I found the courage to turn on the tape recorder.

I carried it down into the living room, of which the windows were open, the year being now once again well advanced into spring. It was twilight, and I turned on all the lamps.

After a whir of scratches and laughing whispers began some absurd dialogue Carol had picked up between Mrs. Brodhag and me, without our knowing it, about leaking eaves and how they should be got at. "You might as well be married the way she nags you," Carol said into the machine she had herself initiated with this prank. Then followed some of her piano pieces, including the Chopin *Nocturne* I had managed to get on the tape the night of the unfortunate television program. I stood at the window with a heavy drink as each molten note dropped out of nowhere onto my heart. There was a long silence after the music, and I was about to end the entertainment as a poor idea when my hand was arrested at the switch by the sound of her voice. This time she read a selection to which she had a few words of preface:

"I want you to know that everything is all right, Daddy. I mean you mustn't worry, really. You've helped me a lot — more than you can imagine. I was digging around in the cabinet part at the bottom of the bookshelves for something to read that you would like. I mean, not something from your favorite books of poetry and all, but something of your own. What did I come across but that issue of the magazine put out by your alma mater, with the piece in it about your philosophy of life. Do you remember it? I might as well say that I know what's going on. What you wrote gives me courage to face whatever there is that's coming, so what could be more appropriate than to read it for you now? Remember when you explained it to me? Obviously, I don't understand it all, but I think I get the drift:

"I believe that man must learn to live without those consolations called religious, which his own intelligence must by now have told him belong to the childhood of the race. Philosophy can really give us nothing permanent to believe either; it is too rich in answers, each canceling out the rest. The quest for Meaning is foredoomed. Human life 'means' nothing. But that is not to say that it is not worth living. What does a Debussy *Arabesque* 'mean,' or a rainbow or a rose? A man delights in all of these, knowing himself to be no more — a wisp of music and a haze of dreams dissolving against the sun. Man has only his own two feet to stand on, his own human trinity to see him through: Reason, Courage, and Grace. And the first plus the second equals the third."

241

I reached the couch at last, on which I lay for some hours as though I had been clubbed, not quite to death. I wished that pound of gristle in my breast would stop its beating, as once in the course of that night I think it nearly did. The time between the last evening songs of the birds and their first cries at daybreak was a span of night without contents, blackness as stark as the lights left burning among the parlor furniture. Sometime towards its close I went to my bedroom, where from a bureau drawer I drew a small cruciform trinket on a chain. I went outside, walking down the slope of back lawn to the privet hedge, over which I hurled it as far as I could into the trees beyond. They were the sacred wood where we had so often walked, looking for the first snowdrops, listening for peepers, and in the clearings of which we had freed from drifts of dead leaves the tender heads of early violets.

I looked up through the cold air. All the stars were out. That pit of jewels, heaven, gave no answer. Among them would always be a wraith saying, "Can't I stay up a little longer?" I hear that voice in the city streets or on country roads, with my nose in a mug of cocoa, walking in the rain or standing in falling snow. "Pick one out and follow it to the ground."

How I hate this world. I would like to tear it apart with my own two hands if I could. I would like to dismantle the universe star by star, like a treeful of rotten fruit. Nor do I believe in progress. A vermin-eaten saint scratching his filth in the hope of heaven is better off than you damned in clean linen. Progress doubles our tenure in a vale of tears. Man is a mistake, to be corrected only by his abolition, which he gives promise of seeing to himself. Oh, let him pass, and leave the earth to the flowers that carpet the earth wherever he explodes his triumphs. Man is inconsolable, thanks to that eternal "Why?" when there is no Why, that question mark twisted like a fishhook in the human heart. "Let there be light," we cry, and only the dawn breaks.

What are these thoughts? They are the shadow, no doubt, reaching out to declare me my father's son. But before that I shall be my daughter's father. Not to say my brother's brother. Now through the meadows of my mind wander hand in hand Louie and Carol and at last little Rachel, saying, "My grace is sufficient for thee." For we are indeed saved by grace in the end — but to give, not take. This, it seems then, is my Book of the Dead. All I know I have learned from them — my long-suffering mother and my crazy father, too, and from Greta, gone frowning somewhere, her secret still upon her brow. All I am worth I got from them. And Rena too, and Dr. Simpson's little boy, whom I never saw. What was his name? Stevie. "A dolphin boy," the doctor had said, in trying to describe him to me. I sometimes see him when I'm out walking on my lunch hour in New York, wading through the pigeons beside the defunct fountain in Bryant Park, behind the library. "Can't I stay up a little longer?"

I could not decline the burden of resumption. The Western Gate is closed. That exit is barred. One angel guards it, whose sword is a gold head smiling into the sun in a hundred snapshots. The child on the brink of whose grave I tried to recover the faith lost on the edge of my brother's is the goalkeeper past whom I can now never get. In the smile are sealed my orders for the day. One has heard of people being punished for their sins, hardly for their piety. But so it is. As to that other One, whose voice I thought I heard, I seem to be barred from everything it speaks in comfort, only the remonstrance remaining: "Verily I say unto thee, Thou shalt by no means come out thence, till thou hast paid the uttermost farthing."

I went inside and brewed some coffee. It seemed feat enough not to reach for another beverage, even at that early hour. The stars had paled and day was breaking. As I sat waiting for the pot to boil, I thought that later in the morning I would telephone the Steins in Trenton and ask about Rachel. I hoped the 6-MP would take her a long way, till school started again, at least. That was always the most important milestone among us parents, Going Back to School. More than making another Christmas, somehow. It didn't take a wise man to understand why. That's the one thing we never stop doing: Going Back to School.

As I sat in the kitchen drinking the coffee, I set my mind to the problem of taking Rachel something of Carol's without letting on anything. Down in the garden amid the lilacs' wasted scent the bees hummed and the hummingbirds shot. It would be a clear morning. The sun had poured its first light through the trees below the garden, gilding the papered wall. The glance directed by the new owners at its ranks of yellow stripes and clumps of bruised fruit gave assurance that this paper would soon be coming down. Truth to tell, we had never liked it much ourselves. There were distant sounds of neighbors stirring, starting the day. An early riser called to someone in the farm below the trees. A wood thrush sang in the merciless summer boughs.

Sometime later, there was a footstep on the path and a knock on the door. It was Omar Howard, come to say good morning and to ask if I had found the Egyptian scarab ring of Carol's, which I had promised him. I had indeed, and, pressing it into his hand, received in return a volume I might find of interest — *Zen: The Answer?*

I sat paging through it for a few minutes after he had gone, sampling what would be perused at more leisure later. ". . . detached attachment . . . roll with nature . . . embrace her facts so as not to be crushed by them . . . swim with the . . . " And of course the Chinese original of that invisible wall-motto in the hospital corridor: "No fuss." On the jacket was a picture of the author, seen trimming a gardenia bush, his hobby. I boarded a train to California, in one or another of whose hanging gardens the wise man dwelt, and, bearding him there, asked whether there were any order of wisdom by which the sight of flowers being demolished could be readily borne. "Watch," I said, and tore from a branch the most perfect of his blossoms and mangled it into the dirt with my heel. Then I tore another, then another, watching studiously his expression as I ground the white blooms underfoot . . .

These thoughts were cut short with the reminder that I must write a letter of recommendation for Omar to a prep school he was trying to get into, for which I had also promised to kick in a little tuition money, if memory served.

Time heals nothing — which should make us the better able to minister. There may be griefs beyond the reach of solace, but none worthy of the name that does not set free the springs of sympathy. Blessed are they that comfort, for they too have mourned, may be more likely the human truth. "You had a dozen years of perfection. That's a dozen more than most people get," a man had rather sharply told me one morning on the train. He was the father of one of Carol's classmates, a lumpish girl of no wiles and no ways, whose Boston mother had long since begun to embalm her dreams in alcohol. I asked him to join me sometime in a few beers and a game or two at the bowling alleys, where one often saw him hanging about alone. He agreed. Once I ran into Carol's teacher, Miss Halsey. "Some poems are long, some are short. She was a short one," Miss Halsey had summed up, smiling, with the late-Gothic horse face which guarantees that she will never read any poems, long or short, to any children of her own. Again the throb of compassion rather than the breath of consolation: the recognition of how long, how long is the mourners' bench upon which we sit, arms linked in undeluded friendship, all of us, brief links, ourselves, in the eternal pity.